Who, what, where, when, die

By Amanda M. Lee

Table of Contents

One

I was shot at by a guy in lederhosen when I was a teenager. True story.

My friends and I were playing basketball after dark in the high school parking lot -- a regular occurrence to cut down on the perpetual boredom that accompanies growing up in the world's smallest town -- when he arrived.

At first, we didn't think much of him. Yeah, he was wearing lederhosen, but this was the backwoods of Michigan, not New York, and fashion isn't a big thing in Michigan so we just kind of accepted it. Big mistake.

Our Michigan yodeler -- who was only wearing lederhosen mind you, no shirt, no shoes, no underwear (yeah, they were that short) -- was apparently also tanked and decided the only thing better than his buzz would be our basketball and a buzz.

He circled us silently, while watching us as carefully as someone who couldn't walk a straight line possibly could. He was close enough for us to smell the intoxicating combination of Old Spice and Milwaukee's Best when it happened.

He darted in, stole our ball as it rimmed off after an errant shot, and immediately sprinted away into the encompassing darkness.

We all stood there for a minute in surprised silence when one of the guys with me suddenly yelled, "Get him!"

So, in our infinite teenage wisdom, we all decided it was a great idea to chase an almost naked, grimy guy who smelled like the world's worst hangover and follow him off the court and into the foliage-laden darkness that surrounded the school.

Now, as the only girl playing with the boys I wasn't quite as fast, so I was a few steps behind. I was momentarily scared out of my wits when a dark figure came running back from the direction everyone had just fled and barreled into me -- knocking me on my ass.

"He's got a gun. Run!"

Now, I'm not one for being bossed around by boys (or anyone for that matter), but I decided to swallow my women's lib and listen for a change when a loud shot rang out. Apparently, the hills weren't alive with the sound of music -- but gunfire.

I didn't need any further encouragement. I ran. Not for my car -- which was out in the open and under a bright streetlight -- but for downtown and safety. I ran the three blocks to the police station and, much to my chagrin, the only cop on duty in our three-cop town was also the town's biggest jerk.

"Let me get this straight," he said, while brushing down the porn mustache he'd been grooming since the 1970s and taking in our red-rimmed eyes and the faint smell of pot in the air that mingled with our fear. "You're saying a guy in lederhosen stole your basketball and shot at you?"

I'm telling you, the guy was a loser.

"Why would we make that up?"

"Maybe you're just . . . confused," he countered, as he tried to lecherously look down my tank top. "That's what happens when you smoke pot, you know."

Of course we knew. The funny thing was, so did he since he sold to half the town, but that probably wasn't the argument to make at the time.

Luckily for us, no argument was necessary. It seems our lederhosen-clad drunk had decided to make a cameo downtown -- sans our basketball but with his shotgun.

We all decided on the spot to chalk the basketball up as a loss we probably didn't want back given that lederhosen guy was doubly armed. He had his gun in one hand and his own personal pistol in the other and both were fully pumped, if you know what I mean.

So it was no surprise that now, a full ten years later, I wasn't awed by the similar sight in front of me as a 300-pound bearded wonder danced in the second story window of an apartment complex with a hand gun in one hand and his own small pistol in the other. He too was naked and, um, double fisting it.

Despite being safely entrenched behind police barricades, unfortunately my eyes were being assailed by the hairy beast -- and his little bald friend.

I turned to the cop standing next to the barricade to lodge my complaint.

"Can't you guys make him put on some shorts or something?"

The cop gave me a dirty and pointed look. "Everyone needs to move across the street -- including media."

I debated pushing the subject, but given my disdain of law enforcement, I merely shrugged and moved to the other side of the road, where I proceeded to plop down in the shade to watch the unfolding show.

My name is Avery Shaw, and for the past five years I'd been working as a local news reporter for the Macomb Monitor in Michigan. I was fully aware that a barricaded gunman on a hot summer day had the potential to last hours -- until the cops either broke down the door and shot the guy with rubber bullets or he passed out from his own alcohol consumption. They very rarely ended with actual shots fired by the gunman.

The Monitor is the county paper in Macomb, a northern suburb of Detroit, which boasts a large redneck community, and a nice view of Canada when looking across Lake St. Clair.

I sighed, wishing I'd thought to bring a magazine to amuse myself with while I waited for the show to play out. I had only been sitting there for a few minutes when I noticed a car pull up to the curb next to me, and a distraught looking woman get out.

I figured right away that this must be a family member -- his mother I guessed -- since I doubted that anyone would want to actually climb into bed with Grizzly Adams on a regular basis.

I got to my feet and made my way over to the woman, pasting my best fake "you can trust me" smile on my face.

"Ma'am, do you know him?" I asked, gesturing to the figure in the second story apartment that was now jamming to "Baby Got Back" while flopping around. Ugh, it was worse when he gyrated, if that was possible. It was like there were a thousand little bugs trying to jump out of his fat rolls.

The woman, who looked to be in her late 60s, narrowed her eyes as she took in my denim Capris and "I did it all for the Wookie" tank top. "Who are you?"

I introduced myself and handed her a card to prove who I was. She still looked dubious. "They let you dress like that for work?"

I tucked my shoulder length blonde hair behind my ear and debated how to answer the question. Truth was, I wasn't supposed to be dressed like this but the editors at the paper pretty much let me do whatever I wanted to do rather than argue with me. I can get shrill when the situation demands it.

I opted to ignore her statement, especially given that fashion advice from a woman wearing a pink Hawaiian muumuu wasn't on the top of my "to do" list for the day.

"Does he do this often?" It seemed like a legitimate question and, when in doubt, it doesn't hurt to distract the person you're trying to squeeze information from.

The woman shifted her eyes off me and took in her rotund son. Her expression didn't betray whatever was going on in her mind. For a second I found it ridiculous that she would dare veto my outfit when her own son couldn't even bother to put on his dirty tighty whities, but I decided to keep those thoughts to myself. I'm nothing if not professional.

"He's just upset," she said. "Bart's not hurting anyone. He would never hurt anyone. He's the kindest man in the world." Except for the visual assault on my eyes. "He lost his job recently. He worked for the DPW. This is really the county's fault."

Like most communities in Michigan, Macomb was suffering under severe financial deficits and had to make deep cuts in manpower in recent years. It was no surprise to me that someone would be upset about losing a cushy county job at the public works department. His way of coping seemed dubious to me, though.

"I understand the drinking, but why does he have to do it naked . . . and with a gun?"

His mother glared at me. "He's just upset. This isn't a big deal. The gun is registered and people are allowed to be naked in their own home."

I thought about it a second. "So why didn't he just shut the curtains?"

His mother sighed deeply -- one of those long suffering gestures that every mother seems hardwired with once they hit the age of forty -- and looked down at her shoes and then at mine. I doubted my blue toenails and cutesy flip-flops with little martinis all over them were doing much to prove to this lady that I was trustworthy.

"Don't you have anything better to do than ruin my son's life? You reporters are like rats. You're no better than rats." Her hands were shaking around the handle of her too large paisley purse. For a second, I was worried she would try to hit me with it.

"Well, I guess I'm in the right neighborhood," I responded, as I took in the rundown cul de sac in

Eastpointe. Years ago, Eastpointe was better known as East Detroit, but in an effort to distance themselves from the city, they tried to rebrand themselves. Now they were known as a community that had a severe rat problem because there were so many abandoned houses. The rats in the local government were just as rampant.

I'd actually meant it as an offhand comment but the naked rapper's mother didn't seem to see it that way.

"You just see yourself so much better than us don't you little miss high and mighty," she spat. Then she dumped the cup of coffee she was carrying on my very cute little flip-flops.

Now, I'll put up with a lot, but no one messes with my shoes. I've got a shoe fetish to match Carrie Bradshaw's on *Sex and the City*, only I like cute and practical shoes that I can actually wear in public and don't make me look like a streetwalker.

Before I could respond to the old woman who'd ruined my shoes, I felt a strong presence move in to the rear of me and put an arm around my chest to restrain me back against a ridiculously solid chest.

"Mrs. Harrison, I'm Sheriff Farrell," a gravelly voice said from behind me. "Won't you please move over to the barricades? There's an officer there that wants to set it up so you can try and talk to your son."

The woman nodded curtly at the sheriff, flashing him a thankful look before shooting one more glare at me, and moved away. Looked like my world famous personal skills had hit another home run.

"You just can't behave yourself, can you?"

I removed the leanly muscled arm from around my neck, turned around and came face to face with Jake Farrell, the sheriff of Macomb County. He was also my high school boyfriend.

"Jake," I said stiffly as I took in his dark black hair, which was pushed high on his forehead in a messy bird's nest. His lean features -- highlighted by ludicrously rich brown eyes that resembled a yummy chocolate bar -- regarded me with a mixture of amusement and anger. "She started it," I offered lamely.

"Yeah, and I'm sure you had no hand in it whatsoever."

I pursed my lips as I debated how to respond. Jake and I had a tortured past. In high school I thought I loved him -- of course I thought I loved Zima about that time too, so there's no accounting for taste. He was two years older than me and had a knack for showing me a good time -- including talking me out of my panties on a regular basis. We got in a lot of trouble with one another over our teen years, the highlight of which resulted in his arrest for urinating on a 9-foot fiberglass fish -- and the cop who tried to stop him -- in an adjacent town.

His father, the county sheriff, didn't take our youthful enthusiasm the same way my parents did. I was merely grounded for two weeks, warned about the risks of talking to a cop without a lawyer present and lectured on the finer points of private urination. He was strongly encouraged to join the Army.

We kept in touch a couple times a month for the next few years. After all, I still had two years of high school left and my popularity was now cemented thanks to the fish incident. However, once I went to college the letters dwindled, mostly on my side, and I was introduced to a whole smorgasbord of new men. I enjoyed the expansive buffet.

Given the riffraff I spent my time with in college, sometimes I wondered if it was a mistake to lose touch with Jake. At times like this, though, I knew it was the best decision I'd ever made.

After his military stint -- where I'd heard he'd excelled in elite operations -- Jake came home to be a cop about an hour south of where his father now served as sheriff. When his father died a few years ago, he became the youngest sheriff Macomb County ever had -- running on his father's name, which was well known across the state. For all intents and purposes, however, Jake was something of a rare thing in my book -- a good cop.

I went on to be the bane of existence to cops -- good or bad -- a nosy reporter. While I knew, in my heart, Jake had good intentions and really wanted to do something to help the community, that didn't change my overall impression of cops in general. My philosophy, when dealing with law enforcement, is that they're all control freaks and egomaniacs. These are men that need to control everything around them -- and I don't like being controlled.

"What are you doing here anyway?" I asked, opting to divert rather than engage in some petty bickering match that would result in me losing my temper and possibly being locked in the back of a police cruiser for the umpteenth time. "Isn't this a local issue? Why is the sheriff's department even here?"

"They needed the SWAT team," he simply said.

"That doesn't explain why you're here."

"I'm here to make sure everything goes smoothly," he replied. Jake had a knack for looking through you, even while talking to you.

I smirked in response. "I think you're here because you know that the television crews will show up for the noon report and you want your TV time."

Jake just smiled benignly. "Are you insinuating I'm a media whore?"

I harrumphed as his dimples came out to play. They were my weak point. "I think you like press -- whether it's good or bad."

"I guess you're just my enabler then, huh?"

"Well, on the record Sheriff Farrell, how long do you expect this to go on? Are you going to wait him out or go in guns blazing? You could try peeing on him. I hear that's a real crowd pleaser." Sometimes I speak before I think. It's a gift.

Jake narrowed his eyes as he regarded me. I couldn't tell if he was amused or aggravated by my comment.

"Well, Ms. Shaw, it's not the sheriff's department's job to inform the media of tactics. When the situation has resolved itself, we'll be more than happy to fax you a press release." Yep, he was aggravated.

With those words, he brusquely turned from me and walked across the street to rejoin his uniform clad brethren.

I guess I'd just been dismissed. At least I'd gotten off better than the trout.

Two

After waiting it out in the stifling heat for more than an hour, I gave up waiting for hairy Bart Harrison to come out and decided to return to the office. I wasn't sure if a suburban yeti existed, but I was starting to wonder. If it did, apparently, it danced to bad nineties rap music with a gun and a small wang. It also couldn't hold a beat.

I'd already talked to neighbors, who gave the standard "he was a quiet guy. I never would have expected it." And, despite his attitude, I had Jake's cell phone number, which he always answered, whatever the time. He was the rare breed of an accessible politician -- something than was considered an urban myth by most constituents.

The Monitor is located in Mount Clemens, the county seat of Macomb. It's actually a nice location within spitting distance of the sometimes beautiful and sometimes polluted Clinton River, within driving distance of the courthouse and sheriff's department and within walking distance of good coffee.

Now most people think that being a reporter is some glamorous job. They think it's all important people and important stories. If you've ever had to write boring millage stories while handling eight obits and three glorified rewrites of press releases you'd quickly realize it's not. Everything is relative.

I parked at the building, which was conveniently located next to the closest thing Mount Clemens had to a ghetto -- an area that at one time had been open and beautiful but was now frequented by drug dealers and prostitutes. Ironically, years before, the building had been erected on a dumpsite. Nice huh?

I entered the building, greeting the plump and pleasing secretary Rosa as I went and key fobbed my way through the security doors. The security wasn't really necessary, but I guess someone felt the need to pretend it was. It was implemented a couple of years before when some moron started flying the Iraqi flag right after the two towers fell and started writing all of us individual letters spouting on about the tyranny of the American government and how the media was responsible for all the deaths in Iraq. Personally, I didn't think the nut jobs trying to get into the building were any worse than the nut jobs that already worked there -- but that was just me.

The building isn't overly large, but it is segregated. Classified advertising, retail advertising, editorial, photo, circulation and the back shop all had their own areas. Ironically, being in a gossipy business, we all remained pretty closed off from one another. I didn't know the names of more than half of the advertising staff -- and I liked it that way. The last thing I need to hear about is what their kid did last night and how their husbands hadn't satisfied them since the first Bush had been in office. If I wanted to know what kids did -- and what husbands didn't do -- I'd partake in both.

Reporters are a curious bunch. I've come to the conclusion that, for the most part, the occupation breeds loners. As an only child, that fit my personality perfectly. I don't tend to like people -- whoever they are. I have friends mind you, but I don't need to surround myself with a lot of them and their inane chatter.

When I entered the newsroom I did so via the longer route, which weaved through several empty conference rooms and came in through the back, so as not to run in to my editor. While he'd long ago given up trying to change the way I dressed, it didn't stop him from doing his trademark sigh and annoyed wave-off. His patent response was "Avery, you don't know." It was grating, whether he was talking about my stories or my apparel.

I made my way to my cubicle. Now, it's important to note, that in the reporter section we had full walled cubicles (compared to the lower ones in the advertising department and on the copy desk) to cut down on our incessant talking. Apparently we were a chatty bunch. The only thing the cubicles managed to do was make us take our gossiping out into the main walkway between the cubicles -- something the editors pretended not to see.

"Hey bonehead."

I smiled to myself as I turned to greet my favorite friend at the paper. Marvin Potts is a 50-year-old newsaholic. He lives and breathes all things news and he's proud of it. He watches every local newscast daily (sometimes twice) -- and he sleeps with a police scanner under his pillow. He's got an abrasive personality (which he acknowledges) and somehow, despite that, he always gets the story.

"Hey asshat," I congenially greeted him back.

"Fish is going to have a heart attack if he sees that outfit," Marvin said, referring to our editor Fred Fish. The irony of that statement was that Potts never took time to think about his own outfit. Marvin, as always, was clad in his "uniform." It consisted of black polyester pants, a white cotton button-down shirt, black suspenders, white athletic socks and white tennis shoes from whatever clearance rack he managed to find them on. I'd seen him in it everyday, so I no longer even noticed it unless really pressed -- like when he'd screwed some waitress and then dumped her on sight, pushing her to fling mustard all over his black pants.

"Fish has bigger things to worry about," I responded as I slipped into my cubicle and pulled out my notebook.

Everyone's cubicles are decorated to their own taste at The Monitor. Marvin's is decked out with Shania Twain and boxing photographs. The old pervert at the end who wears his pants four inches too short and self masturbates with change in his pocket has that dark-haired chick from *Desperate Housewives* everywhere. The Polish shyster who always tries to put one over on everyone has mirrors throughout his so he can see when the editor is coming down the aisle and he can pretend he's actually working instead of doing just about anything else.

Me? Mine is tastefully done in a *Star Wars* motif on one wall and Spanish tennis star Rafael Nadal on the other. I like all sports, but tennis is my favorite, and I have an unhealthy crush on the Mallorcan wonder. I'd rather do him than Han Solo, that's how serious my crush is.

Currently, I had a choice, I could get ahead of the game and write the majority of my story and just wait for the press release to confirm it or I could go chat with my co-workers. It was a tough choice but, ultimately, I decided to go get the office gossip.

I lucked out, because the editors were in the budget meeting for the day (where they meet to decide what stories go where in the paper). I smiled as I walked up to my friend Erin's desk. Erin works for the features department and is nothing like me. She's 4'11 inches (compared to my 5'6). She's got short curly hair (think Marsha Clark in the OJ Simpson trial) compared to my straight golden blonde locks (which come from a bottle). She always dresses appropriately. And, the biggest difference is, she's extremely nice.

"Hey Erin, what's going on?"

She greeted me with a delicate smile on her ultra pale features and a shy glance that probably had never laid eyes on a naked man. Ever. "Wow, you're tan. Did you get most of that today?"

I looked down at my decidedly darker skin and shrugged. "Guess so. I guess it was a trade off. On one hand, I had to watch the world's ugliest man dance naked. On the other, I look so much hotter. Who knew? So anything fun going on today?"

Here's the thing. Erin is the nicest girl ever but she does have one flaw. She loves to gossip. This, of course, benefits me because I have many flaws and one of them is that I, too, love to gossip. Before she could respond, though, an unwelcome guest interrupted.

"Well, well, well, look who has nothing to do as usual? Maybe I should talk to Fish about increasing your workload. They always say the day goes by faster when you have more to do."

I didn't turn to greet the newcomer. I knew who it was by the sound of his annoying rat voice, copy editor Duncan Marlow, aka the office tool.

"What Duncan? You took time away from your busy Civil War reenactment chat room to come and talk with lowly us?"

There are no words to explain Duncan. He's just . . . psycho. He's one of those people that can tick off everyone in the room and yet actually believes that it's you, not him. I once read that's a sign of insanity. In Duncan's case, I agree.

"I'll have you know that Civil War reenactments are cultural events. They are important to remember our heritage. Someone like you would never understand that. Just because they don't dress up like stormtroopers doesn't mean they're boring. This is real life. This is history. Real people lost their lives in the Civil War, not CGI people."

Oh, yeah, Duncan thinks he's the smartest man in the room. In reality, he ranks in the bottom third.

"I think they're just havens for latent homosexuals to polish their guns and get off on seeing each other in frilly outfits," I responded. Now, I just want to point out that I'm not homophobic. I just hate Duncan and he's one of those guys that is constantly bashing gay people -- yet watches the love scene in *Brokeback Mountain* over and over again -- so I went for the easy dig.

"I don't know why you feel the need to sexually harass me," he complained, as he ran his hand through his shortly cropped brown hair. Did I mention he thinks he looks like Tom Cruise? Which is both untrue and disturbing. I fully expect Duncan to jump up on his desk one day like a moron -- of course Oprah won't be there to diffuse the situation.

"Trust me Duncan, no one here wants to have sex with you," I replied, turning my back to dismiss him.

"We'll see what human resources has to say about that," he huffed and walked away.

I wasn't really worried about Duncan turning me in to human resources. He'd done it numerous times before. It was his way. My usual punishment came in the form of a sit-down with the big editor -- on the rare occasion when he actually showed up to work once every two weeks -- and get told, "just don't talk to that asshole." Like I said, I don't like to be bossed around.

Before I could return to gossiping with Erin, the editorial assistant delivered a piece of paper to me that happened to be the press release I was waiting for on the barricaded gunman. Good news, he passed out and the cops took him away without incident. Called that one.

I returned to my desk, cranked out my story and decided to call it a day. At least this way I could go home and play video games for a couple hours before I had to go to bed.

I live in a city called Roseville. It's south of Mount Clemens but well north of Detroit. I have a simple one story, two-bedroom house with hardwood floors and a lot of clutter. Not *Hoarders* clutter, but still, I have my fair share.

My neighborhood is decidedly white trash but entertaining.

On the far end of the street, about ten guys live in one small house and run a chop shop out of the garage. They have two loud and annoying dogs, but the guys who live there are also friendly and mind their own business. They also pushed my car out of a snowdrift last winter – so I actually like them.

On my right is a family who I have never talked to, despite living next to them for three years. Their kids shot an arrow into my house one time, but I just ignored it rather than be forced to introduce myself to them. They get odd visitors at all hours of the night -- except they all go in through the back sliding glass-doors -- even in the dead of winter. I'm pretty sure, given the look of the people who visit, they're dealers.

Across the road from me, three new young guys moved in to a house that weirdly looks like a barn. They're white but they think they're black gangsters -- which is wholly annoying. They talk like they live in the ghetto of Detroit, their pants are always falling off their asses and they have big trucks with those aggravating neon running lights underneath them. I try to pretend they don't exist – which rarely works.

The best feature of my house is that it has one of those huge old style front porches that I have a little bistro table set up on. I like to sit out there and contemplate life – okay, I'm a stress smoker, but I do contemplate some things while sitting out there polluting my lungs.

Today, however, it was the people in the house on my left that were going to be my neighborhood annoyance for the day.

The abode adjacent to my driveway is a two-bedroom ranch that houses a set of unruly brothers, the wife of one of the brothers and a toddler. The wife is extra chatty and the brothers are extra boozy.

Today, the wife was sitting out on her front porch, too. I didn't think I could exit without being ridiculously rude, so I just tried to avoid eye contact with her. She didn't get the hint.

"Did the cops wake you up last night when they were here?"

I was surprised; I had no idea the cops had been here the night before.

"No, why were they here?"

"You know my brother-in-law Larry?"

Of course I knew Larry. He was 55, he constantly tried to talk to me, offered to cook for me, and he had one of those shriveled hand birth defects. It was a case of not wanting to look but not being able to stop looking. Yeah, I'm that awful.

"Yeah, what about Larry?" I asked.

"Have you ever seen the movie *Liar, Liar* with Jim Carrey?"

Hmm, I didn't exactly know where this was going but hey, what the hell.

"Yeah."

"You know the scene in the bathroom where he kicks his own ass?"

"Yeah."

"Well, Larry did that last night."

Come to find out, Larry, on a drunken tear, had beat the living shit out of himself and then called the police and said his brother did it. Seemed he wanted a restraining order so the other brother would have to move out of the house their mother had left them both when she passed away a few years before.

"Huh." What else is there to say to that?

"Instead, Larry injured himself so bad they had to put one of those boot things on him and he's going to be staying in a nursing home for awhile."

Ah, fun times in Roseville.

"Well, that's too bad." Really, what do you say to that? "Well, I've got to go make dinner. See you later."

As I was just about to make my getaway, the white gangsters across the street decided to throw their two cents in.

"Hey, Princess Leia, do you wants to come play with my light saber?" It was the blonde one with the red do-rag who spoke, accentuating his white gangster accent, while thrusting his hips up in a guttural move.

Being a girl who loves *Star Wars*, every guy thinks I wanted to be Princess Leia. If they only knew that I identified more with Han Solo.

"No, but if you don't knock that crap off I'm going to blow your house up like it's the Death Star."

Did I mention I really don't like people?

Three

After three hours of light saber duels on my Nintendo Wii, I fell asleep on the couch that night. My dreams were a jumble of hot sheriffs and naked, hairy fat men doing the rump shaker. I woke up feeling disturbed, by both the naked sheriff and the fat man.

The first order of business was to get the paper. If we didn't get a free subscription, I would probably wait to leaf through it when I got to work -- after all, my meager proceeds from being a reporter usually went for DVDs, video games and shoes.

I opened the front page, which featured my story as the main item with art of the SWAT team mobilizing. Of course, Jake managed to get in the picture. Some things are a constant.

In Macomb County, we could only boast three celebrities (all white rappers) so as far as the residents were concerned, Jake was as good as a Beatle. He just had better hair. Go figure.

As I was reading what everyone else contributed for the day -- Marvin had a hilarious story about a guy getting arrested in Warren for molesting a pumpkin in his back yard in front of the neighbor's kids -- I noticed a piece of notebook paper fall from the center of the paper.

Curious, I opened it, and immediately wished I hadn't. The message was simple and to the point.

If you don't start minding your own business, you'll wish you had.

Hmm, the life of a reporter. I have the nicest fans.

The sad thing is, this isn't the first threat I've ever gotten. In fact, this wasn't the first threat I'd gotten this month. However, this was the first one that arrived in person at my home. Sadly, though, people tend to threaten the welfare of reporters often. They just usually do it on my voicemail at work or the paper's message board.

Since everything was spelled correctly -- a bonus -- I opted to do the sensible thing. I folded the note up, took it into my office, and filed it in my Darth Vader cookie jar. I wasn't totally ignoring it but, most times, people just feel the need to vent and then they're over it.

I showered, watched the ladies on *The View* argue about whether or not *American Idol* had a future and then debated what to do for the day. One thing to note about reporters, you never have good hours. My shifts jump from day to night on a regular basis and, since I'd worked for Marvin the previous Sunday, I had this Friday off.

I had to go to a family dinner later in the night, but I had a good five hours to burn and was debating what to do. I really wanted to jump back into *The Force Unleashed* on my game console, but figured it was such a nice day I should get some exercise instead. Ultimately, the gym was unappealing so I opted for a visit to Metro Beach.

Macomb County is home to many beaches, most pristine, and most you wouldn't want to enter the water at. St. Clair Shores is contaminated with PCBs and many of the other beaches are contaminated on a regular basis with e.coli. Swimming wasn't an option, but people watching always was.

I spent the day eating hot dogs, visiting the Nature Center to say hi to my friend Abby and soaking up the rays on a bench. Before I realized it, it was almost 3:30 p.m. -- and if I expected to make it to the family restaurant in time for dinner, I had to get moving.

Despite being an only child, I have a rather large extended family. They own a diner-style restaurant in a small town about an hour north of the city and every Friday at 5 p.m. whoever can make it congregates for dinner.

The best thing about the family restaurant is the fact that you would never know that gang wars are located only fifty miles away. The town was so small that people forgot about the urban chaos that was so close.

As for family dinners, the rule was, if you can, you're expected to make it. Actually, the only acceptable excuse for missing dinner was arrest or work. Depending on the family member -- both were utilized often.

Truth be known, crazy as they are, I like my family. They're entertaining and no matter how bad my life is at the time, their life is always worse. In essence, it's always good times listening to their weekly travails.

Plus, according to the tersely worded message left on my cell phone by my annoyed mother, my great-grandmother (who generally resides in Florida) would be making a cameo after returning from her honeymoon with her third husband.

If I missed dinner tonight it would be a week of guilt ridden silence and then an angry phone call from my mother. Love the woman, but man she can hold a grudge.

Rather reluctantly, I made my way to the car. I looked in the mirror once I was settled, saw I'd received a lot more sun than I realized, and debated about going home to change my clothes. I knew the *Goonies* "Truffle Shuffle" T-shirt I was wearing, the lack of makeup and the fresh sunburn were all going to be bulls-eyes on my chest when my mother caught sight of them. I weighed which lecture would be worse -- being late or my attire -- and ultimately decided to just suck it up. Truth is, sometimes I like watching my mother's head implode when she sees my outfit. It's just one of the fun games we play.

I immediately jumped on the freeway and started my trek north. I figured I might as well not put it off.

The family restaurant is really a throwback to the 1950s -- which is when my great-grandmother and her first husband opened it after they got married. I call him her first husband instead of my great-grandfather because I really can't remember the man. I have one memory of him playing chess with my uncle Tim, his namesake.

What's interesting about Great-Grandpa Tim is that I always heard he was this mellow dude who was kind of, well, boring. Funny thing is, he died while having sex with my great-grandmother (they were in their sixties at the time, mind you) and when the paramedics came he was stone dead with a stone hard-on. My family was mortified and tried to cover him up with a sheet, but the tent was still obvious. After his death, a long held family secret came out that my great-grandfather had fathered another child out of wedlock -- with my great-grandma's sister. Guess he wasn't that boring after all.

Anyway, after his death, my grandparents Jasper and Tilly took over and now my uncle Tim runs the place -- with unwanted oversight from my Grandpa Jasper. For her part, my great-grandmother Edith moved on to marry a mean man to get his money and now a nice man on his last leg -- who also happens to be rich.

I guess you could say I come from a curious gene pool. The restaurant side of the family is my mother's side of the family. She and my father divorced a few years ago and his family is just as weird -- but in a different way. Oh, and my dad's side of the family can't cook for crap but is uncomfortably tight-lipped while my mom's side of the family are all gourmet cooks and never met a piece of gossip they didn't want to spread. Funny thing is, while the so-called adults in the family get embarrassed by each other's antics, my multitude of cousins and I just find it entertaining and fodder for dinner conversation.

I entered the restaurant, said hi to Eva the waitress, and then made my way to the family booth -- which is always reserved for us. It's one of those long rectangular ones that really isn't big enough to hold the girth of our family, but since everyone gets up and mingles around a lot no one has a problem sitting down to eat.

The first person I saw was my mother, who took one look at my outfit and rolled her eyes in absolute disapproval.

"You go out in public like that?"

I shrugged. "My power suit is at the dry cleaners," I lied. "Where's great-grandma?"

"She isn't here yet," my mother chastised me. "I told you on the phone she wouldn't be here until around six."

Well color me embarrassed -- or annoyed, either one will do.

I decided that I was done talking to my mother for a while and instead slid in to the booth next to my cousin, Derrick. We'd been raised together since we were only a few months apart in age and he was the closest thing I had to a brother. He was also a cop, so while I was glad to see him I was also leery.

"What's up?"

He grunted as he greeted me. That's hello in cop talk. "I talked to Sheriff Farrell today. He told me you were a pain in the ass at that barricaded gunman yesterday." For a second, I flashed to the time when Derrick and I were ten years old and I blackened his eye with a stick while we were ostensibly playing. Then I exhaled slowly to calm my agitation.

"Well, Sheriff Farrell should pull that stick out and get over it," I replied angrily. "I was doing my job."

"Yeah, you're always doing your job and you're always an ass when you're doing it."

Problem was, I really couldn't argue the point. Instead I chose to ignore it.

"Well, someone else obviously didn't like my attitude at the scene either. I got a threat with my morning paper today. I'm assuming it had to do with that story since it's the only one I filed yesterday."

For the first time, Derrick looked at me. "Did they threaten to kill you?"

"Don't sound so hopeful," I said as he grimaced in response. "No, it was just a mind your own business or you'll regret it thing."

Derrick was quiet for a second; he seemed to be choosing his words carefully. "I'm probably going to regret this . . . but maybe you should think about getting a gun."

My eyebrows practically shot off my head.

"A gun? Me? Are you kidding me? I could never shoot someone."

"You wouldn't necessarily have to shoot someone. You could just have it to scare someone. We used to play *G.I. Joe* all the time as a kid and you didn't have a problem shooting me with a paint gun," he reminded me.

"A paint gun can't kill you," I said. "A paint gun just makes you look like an asshat."

Derrick smirked. "You don't need a paint gun to do that. You do that every day you get dressed. *The Goonies*, really? How old are you?"

"Nine months younger than you, and you used to love *The Goonies,* too."

"Yeah, then I hit puberty."

"You hit puberty?" Now this was hitting below the belt. My poor 5'4" cousin always took a ribbing about his height. I think that's why he became a cop. No one argues with a cop, even when he can double for an Oompa Loompa.

Luckily, our petty argument didn't get a chance to escalate because my great-grandmother had chosen that moment to enter with her new husband.

"What's this one's name?" I changed the subject.

"Elroy, I think. She met him at the old folks home. She was painting when he knocked on the door to introduce himself. Let's just say she made an impression."

I smiled to myself. It was well known that, even in her late eighties, my free spirit great-grandmother liked to paint in the nude.

Derrick smiled at the visual too, and then shuddered.

"Hello everyone," she trilled in dramatic fashion, as she twirled in her very bright green muumuu.

Everyone greeted great-grandma Edith with a smile and a kiss on the cheek -- as was expected.

"Oh, Avery, you're sunburned," she said like a typical concerned great-grandmother. "If you look like a tomato, you're never going to get any action. Men don't like outdoorsy girls. They'd rather have sex with girls who keep a clean house and cook a good meatloaf." Not so much like a typical grandmother.

Actually, to be fair, my great-grandmother was probably a very good female role model back in the 1950s. She ran the roost, while her first husband just lived in it. She was famous for her demanding personality -- something I was familiar with.

When my mother was a small child, Great-Grandma Edith would take her and her siblings to the cemetery to steal flower arrangements. One child was to act like a lookout to spot the police while the others gathered enough blooms for the summer. Edith always said the victims of her overt crime were dead, so they wouldn't miss their flowers anyway.

As far as cooking meatloaf, my great-grandmother was a notoriously bad cook, so I didn't know whom she was trying to appease with that comment. I knew it wasn't herself -- or me. Her first husband was the maestro who launched the restaurant with his wonderful cooking. Her contribution to the restaurant was decorating. My personal favorite was a pair of ceramic frogs that she applied makeup and false eyelashes to which still lived in the women's bathroom today. I guess you could say she was eclectic.

Everyone was eating at this point. The sun from the day had pretty much sapped my appetite, so I opted for the restaurant's trademark vegetable soup and a salad -- which I mostly just pushed around my plate.

Chatter was going on around me, so I was lost in my own thoughts when I realized that everyone was not only quiet, but also looking at me. "What?"

"Grandma was asking you a question," my mother didn't look pleased.

"Oh, sorry, what was it?"

"I said, I have a good story for you," she said.

"Oh, yeah, what is that?" Everyone thinks they have a good story. They usually don't.

"Well, on the cruise we went on, they had private unisex saunas."

"Uh, huh." And the "Who Cares?" award goes to?

"Well, Elroy and I decided to try one out and when we went in we were sliding all over the place. When you're naked, and old, you don't want to slide into things because everything is just flopping around and it gets caught on stuff."

Derrick looked horrified. The bacon cheeseburger he was eating actually fell out of his mouth. I wasn't far behind with my own terror. She was painting quite a picture -- one that no one wanted to see. "So what's the story?"

Great-grandma harrumphed. "Well, discrimination against old people, of course. They should have special railings and non-slip flooring. Do you know that people complained about seeing me naked? That's just not right."

There were so many things about this conversation that just weren't right.

I turned to Derrick, whose face was about as red as it could get, as he studiously studied his plate and refused to make eye contact with anyone else at the table for fear of laughing. "I'm thinking that gun might be a good idea after all."

Four

After two hours of dinner, where my Aunt Sally informed everyone in the restaurant that her husband couldn't be present because she'd fractured his penis the previous evening while having sex, I couldn't get out of the restaurant fast enough.

I love my Aunt Sally, I find her hilariously fascinating, but hearing about her redneck husband's penis ailments was giving me the willies. Ironically, this wasn't the first time I'd heard about the sexploits of one of my aunt's husbands. Years ago, she came home to find her first husband in bed with another man. That, too, was an often-told family secret. Too often, if you ask me.

As I made my way back to the city, I let my mind wander back to what Derrick had suggested. A gun. While I really wasn't worried about my safety, the idea of a gun wasn't totally unappealing. Quite frankly, I knew this wouldn't be the final threat I would receive.

I continued to debate the merits of getting a gun for the hour drive back to Macomb County and ultimately decided that at least looking for one wouldn't be such a bad idea. The problem is, I'm an impulse shopper.

I opted to go to a pawnshop in downtown Mount Clemens, which just happened to be right next door to my favorite coffee shop. I decided to get the coffee first and then made my way into the pawnshop, which I'd seen a hundred times but never actually entered.

I don't know what I was expecting, but it wasn't what I saw. I think my ideas of what a pawnshop was supposed to be had been inexplicably shaped by old Miami Vice episodes and that *Pawn Stars* show on the History Channel.

This store was bright, clean and much bigger than it looked from the outside. It also housed some weird ass crap in it. There was a giant wooden Indian – Native American, for the politically correct -- statue right inside the door.

"What the . . . ?"

"Those actually used to be very popular," a voice said from behind me. "They were housed outside tobacco stores during Prohibition times. They're considered antiques now."

I turned to find the source of the history lesson and was surprised to see one of the best looking men I'd ever seen in person. He was about six feet tall, with shoulder length brown hair, clear blue eyes and some of the biggest muscles I'd witnessed outside of a gay gym. He was wearing a white tank top and a red flannel shirt over top of it. The flannel was rolled up high enough to show off a set of Native American tattoos on his forearms. Can you say yum?

I, of course, answered with my hormones. "Thanks for the history lesson." Did I mention when I flirt it comes out snarky?

"I'm Eliot Kane." Mr. Hunk of Burning Love smiled and extended his hand in greeting. Guess he liked snarky.

"Avery Shaw."

"Well, what can I do for you Ms. Shaw?"

Now here was a conundrum. Most men don't like strong women. And a woman who carries a gun? They really don't like that. The problem is, I'm a crappy liar unless it really benefits me. I can lie to a source, no problem, but lying just to lie doesn't usually benefit me. I opted for the truth.

"I'm looking for a gun."

Eliot seemed surprised. "What for?"

"What do you mean what for? Do you ask everyone that comes in what they want a gun for? I bet if I was a man you wouldn't ask me what I wanted a gun for?"

"Actually, I would. I don't tend to just hand over a gun to whoever asks for one. My conscience wouldn't allow it."

"You have a conscience? You own a pawnshop. You take things from people who are desperate and then sell them for a hundred percent markup, and you're worried about what I'm going to do?"

So much for charming his pants off.

Surprisingly, he didn't seem that put off. "Are you always like this?"

"Like what?"

"So aggressive."

My eyebrows practically melded with my hairline. "Me? Aggressive? Let me guess, any woman who doesn't just roll over and bat her eyelashes at you and swoon into your big arms is considered aggressive?"

"No, any woman who comes in with your attitude is aggressive."

Funnily enough, I couldn't really argue with his statement. That didn't stop me from doing it, though.

"Listen, you don't know me so don't pretend that you do," I snapped. "I came in here to do business. You obviously don't need my business, so I'll do it elsewhere." I was all prepared to flounce out in all my glory when Eliot started laughing.

"You just pull shit out of your ass, don't you?"

"What?"

"All you have to do is tell me why you want a gun? Is that so hard?"

"Well, Mr. Nosy, if you must know, I need a gun because I got a threat in my morning paper. I don't plan on shooting anyone, but if people know I have a gun they just might stay away." All right, the truth is, he's too hot to shop somewhere else.

"Why would someone threaten you?"

What is this, Twenty Questions? "I happen to be a reporter for The Monitor. You'd be surprised how many people I piss off on a given week."

"Honey, I think you'd piss just as many people off if you were a cashier," he responded with a throaty laugh. Was he flirting with me? "What kind of gun are you looking for?" He moved down the case and pointed towards the myriad of weapons on display.

I moved down across from him and blew out a sigh. "I don't know. Nothing too big. Something that can fit in my purse. Something that's safe."

"First of all, you can't carry it in your purse without a permit," Eliot said. "And, given your temper, I don't suggest you get that permit. You're road rage waiting to happen if I ever saw it."

"What, you're worried I'll get my period, snap and kill someone?" I think I'd just been insulted.

"I don't think you can help yourself. That's just the way you are." Now Eliot smiled, a warm smile that lit up his entire face, like he was Han Solo or something. "I didn't say it was a bad thing, or that it wasn't a turn-on, I just don't think you want murder on your record. It may infringe on your job performance."

What can I say? When you're right, you're right.

I took in a deep, calming breath. "What do you suggest?"

"Well, I'm thinking a simple revolver will handle your needs," he said. "And maybe a late dinner will handle mine?"

"A revolver huh?" Wait, did he just ask me out? Don't acknowledge it, I warned myself.

"Did you just hit on me?" I don't listen to anyone's advice, even my own.

Eliot laughed. "Is that okay?"

Here's the thing. I like to play the game, but I'm not really good at the dating thing. I think it has to do with my freedom level. I don't like to be told what to do – or when to do it. I made a split second decision.

"How about we compromise?"

He waited for me to continue.

"Yes to the gun and maybe to dinner -- another night. I actually have something going on tonight."

"Oh yeah, what's that? A date with someone else?"

This was a sticky situation. If I lied and said I had a date with someone else he might lose interest. If I told the truth, and owned up to what I was really doing he would definitely lose interest. Like I said, though, I'm a crappy liar.

"Well, if you must know, I'm going to see the *Star Wars* symphony at Independence Hill." How much of a geek am I?

Eliot actually snorted with laughter. "I'm sorry, the *Star Wars* symphony? Is that actually a real thing?"

"Yes, it's a thing!" Now I knew I'd been insulted. "I'll have you know, this show has been sold out for weeks."

"I'm sure it has," Eliot said with a smirk. "Well, how about this? There's a three-day waiting period for the gun. Why don't we revisit dinner when you come back in for it?"

That sounded reasonable, and his smile was practically orgasm inducing. I felt myself melting -- a rare feeling for me.

"I'll take you to Tattooine or something," he just didn't know when to quit. "Maybe you can wear that Princess Leia bikini?"

They always go for the bikini don't they? Every fan boy's wet dream. What an asshole.

Five

After leaving the hot pawnshop owner and his very unattractive attitude I was in quite a snit. Who did this guy think he was? He obviously thought he was God's gift to women. Problem was, he probably was right.

I discarded thoughts of Eliot Kane from my head and perked myself up by jamming to the *Star Wars* soundtrack in the CD player of my car. There is no problem too big to be alleviated by the medal ceremony music from the first *Star Wars*.

Independence Hill is a relatively small concert venue in Sterling Heights. It seats a couple thousand, but it has a nice and cozy feel to it. I found myself quickly putting my encounter with Eliot Kane out of my head in anticipation of some good music.

I pulled into the amphitheater's parking lot, flashed my press credentials -- hey, I'm not paying for parking when I don't have to -- and found a spot with relatively easy access to the exits.

I checked myself out in the mirror and, if possible, I think I'd gotten even redder. Great. I mentally smacked myself for wearing a *Goonies* T-shirt to a *Star Wars* event -- I didn't like to mix my genres. Well, there was nothing I could do about that now.

I got out of the car and took in the environment with a smile. *Star Wars* fans are a relatively unique breed. They're generally men, from the ages of 13 to 35. Any women present -- and there were precious few -- looked like they had been dragged there against their wishes.

"Hey, watch it lady!"

I stumbled into a big black sheet of clothing. Upon pulling back, I realized it was Darth Vader -- or some sexually repressed teenager dressed up like Darth Vader.

"Sorry," I mumbled. "I didn't see you." I don't know how I missed him.

Vader ignored my apology and caught up to his friends, who were dressed up like stormtroopers, and went on his way.

"What is it, asshole day?"

No one answered, of course.

I made my way into the amphitheater and found my optical senses assailed by a flurry of Tattooine inhabitants and whirling light sabers. Great, it was going to be a long night. There's nothing worse than a fan that actually thinks he's a Jedi.

As I moved to the left I ran in to Barry Whitfield, one of the executives of Independence Hill.

"Hey Barry," I said congenially. He was a good source.

"Avery, I guess I shouldn't be surprised," Barry responded. "If anyone loves *Star Wars,* it's you."

"Yeah, I'm nothing if not predictable."

Barry and I made small talk for a few minutes, including a tip that I should go to the Roseville City Council meeting later in the week -- apparently there was going to be a big to-do about a crematorium -- and we said our goodbyes.

"Sorry I couldn't chat longer," he apologized. "I have a feeling it's going to be war between the good guys and bad guys before it's all said and done tonight."

I couldn't help but agree with him. Letting loose thousands of guys in a closed off space with alcohol and plastic light sabers was begging for a couple of head injuries. No matter what age the men were.

I decided to get something to drink to take the edge off. I walked up to the concession stand and ordered a light beer. You know, less calories.

"I don't suppose you'd get one of those for me?"

I turned to find a young kid, probably 18 years old, dressed in Lando Calrissian garb. He was one of the palest teenagers I've ever seen, and he sported bleached-blond hair and pimped out mirrored sunglasses. Great, I sure attract winners.

"I'm sorry?"

"A beer," he said sheepishly. "I forgot my ID at home and these guys don't believe I'm 21. Can you believe that?"

Actually, I could.

"I'm Lando Skywalker by the way."

Of course he was.

"Lando Skywalker? Seriously?"

"Yeah," he said defensively. "I changed my name legally when I turned 18 a few months . . . a few years ago." Nice save Gretzky.

"Well, Lando, I'm sorry, but I'm really not up for contributing to the delinquency of a minor tonight."

I felt someone move in behind me. Great, with my luck it would be a wookie.

"Yeah, Avery Shaw here only follows the rules."

Oh, crap, it was worse than a wookie. I turned around to come face to face with my hot pawnshop owner. You've got to be kidding me! It was definitely asshole day.

"What are you doing here?"

Lando, in his infinite wisdom, took one look at Eliot's expansive and tattooed muscles and wisely walked away, mumbling something about me not knowing Sith.

Eliot smiled at his retreating back. "He knows he's not black right?"

"I think so. You didn't answer my question, what are you doing here?"

"Well, you made it sound like such a fun time, how could I resist? I mean, a whole night of *Star Wars* music, is there anything better?"

No, there's not. I sipped my beer for lack of anything better to do. During the lull, Eliot signaled to the girl at the concession stand to get him a beer, too. Her flirty smile and flirty attitude with him was annoying. Then, something hit me.

"Hey, how did you get in? This concert has been sold out for weeks?"

Eliot merely smiled. "I have my ways."

If I had to guess, his ways included sweet-talking the teenage girl collecting the tickets by flexing for her. For a second I felt jealous of the girl.

"So, where are we sitting?"

We? "I'm not sitting anywhere. My ticket is for the lawn. I'm standing." I silently hoped he would take that as a hint. Okay, part of me hoped that. The other part desperately wanted to see his light saber.

"So, where are we standing? We don't have much of a view from here."

I didn't want to admit there was nothing to see. Instead, I turned and started making my way up the hill with Eliot following lackadaisically behind. I had the distinct sense he was laughing at me. Nothing could make this moment more humiliating.

"Avery."

Whoops, I was wrong.

Jake, dressed in his uniform per usual, made his way from the entrance to the concert and over to me. He openly smiled, flashing those damn dimples. "I figured you'd be here."

"Only because the *Star Trek* symphony is out of town," Eliot quipped from behind me as I cringed. This was about to get uncomfortable.

Jake turned his attention from me to Eliot -- and he didn't look happy. Perversely, that gave me an extended thrill.

"Kane," Jake said stiffly.

"Sheriff Farrell."

"You guys know each other?"

Neither man responded immediately. They also, I noticed, didn't shake hands in greeting. Interesting.

Finally, Jake, ever the politician, broke the tension.

"Mr. Kane and I were in special forces in the Army together for a brief period. It was a long time ago."

"It was seven years ago," Eliot corrected.

"That's a lifetime ago."

Hmm.

"Well, we should find where we're standing," Eliot smirked condescendingly at Jake.

Jake looked abashed. "You're here together."

"Yes."

"No!" I practically yelled. "We just met tonight and happened to run in to each other here, too." It wasn't exactly a lie. It wasn't exactly the truth either.

Jake wasn't buying it. "Well, I'll leave you two alone then." Was he mad? He sounded mad.

Luckily, things didn't get a chance to get any more awkward as the beating sound of the *Star Wars* theme managed to overtake the entire amphitheater, eliciting a huge cheer from fan boys everywhere.

I turned to see what was going on and noticed that a small crowd in front of the orchestra seemed to be fighting. From the looks of it, the Rebel Alliance was having none of the Imperial Guard. Go figure.

Jake look annoyed.

"Fucking idiots. It never ends." He quickly moved off to gather some men to break up the fight. Problem was, it didn't look like he had enough men. Crap, I had a feeling my *Star Wars* night was about to be ruined.

"I think we should move away from here." Eliot didn't look overtly worried, more like placidly concerned.

Too late. A large guy dressed as a Gamorean Guard (one of those green pig guards from Jabba's Palace, for the uninformed) tumbled into him. Some how, Eliot managed to keep on his feet, but the guard wasn't so lucky. He bounced off Eliot and crashed to the ground. Unfortunately for him, apparently latex wasn't easy to stand up in. He was on the ground flopping like an upended turtle.

"Are you all right?" I figured the latex probably cushioned his fall. I bent over with the intention of helping him up.

"No bitch, I'm not alright. I'm going to sue your boyfriend." So much for helping him up.

"He is not my boyfriend. I barely know him." Nothing wrong with clarification. "Besides that, you ran into him. How is that his fault?"

I didn't get a chance to hear his response. With one smooth move Eliot had grabbed me by my waist and whisked me to the side as group of exuberant Jedis moved past us. All I could focus on in that minute pressed up against him was how rock hard his body was. Man, I am sick.

Things were quickly degenerating -- which meant I was no longer a mere watcher, I was working. It gave me an excuse to try and forget about Eliot's body, which I reluctantly pulled away from. It wasn't easy.

"I'm going to have to cover this," I said ruefully. "It's not everyday you get an alien war in Macomb County."

"Fuckin' Aye," Eliot laughed.

An hour later, I'd gotten quotes from everyone that I needed to, including an enraged Sheriff Farrell who said they'd confiscated more than a hundred light sabers -- and he didn't think they'd bring much at auction.

"This is just bullshit. You *Star Wars* freaks are just nuts."

The paper had heard about the melee and dispatched a photographer -- Jared Jackson, a fun guy in his late forties who was clearly gay but covered up for it by talking gratuitously about female genitalia to anyone who would listen.

"Any Princess Leias in the gold bikini?" he asked, before moving in to do his shooting. Fricking Princess Leia. I noticed that Jared had already managed to find one, with a pretty impressive rack. He was using his telephoto lens -- even though he didn't need it given the celestial globes hanging in his face.

Eliot was still hanging around, but he hadn't talked to me while I conducted interviews. Instead he lounged against the entryway, smiling at any girl who was escorted out in front of him. He smiled even wider at the ones wearing cuffs. I walked over to him to say my goodbyes, while mentally bitch slapping him for being a dog.

"Listen, I have to file this story," I said. He merely nodded. "Sorry you didn't get to hear the show."

This drew a smile from him. "Something tells me I'll get another chance if I spend much more time with you." He waved goodbye and left for the parking lot.

I had a feeling, too, that I was getting in way over my head.

Six

I slept in the next day. Surprisingly, light saber battles take it out of you. I leisurely got out of bed, slipped on my comfy Yoda slippers and padded into the kitchen.

You would think, coming from a restaurant family and having worked in the family business throughout my teen years, I would be a good cook. You would be wrong. I can barely boil water and brown toast.

I opted for my usual -- a bowl of Fruity Pebbles and a large glass of tomato juice. Breakfast is the most important meal of the day, after all. I shoved my copy of *The Goonies* into the DVD player to entertain myself during breakfast and distract myself from the events of the night before.

Since I had the day off, I figured it was a perfect time to catch up with my best friend Carly, so I jumped in the shower and gave her a call, seeing if she wanted to meet up. Since she was knee deep in wedding preparations -- for a wedding that was still months away, mind you -- she told me I could come over to her parents' house and help her with a seating chart.

Fun for her. Torture for me.

Since I had a distinct lack of anything else to do, though, I opted for an afternoon of torture with Carly and her crazy family. And when I say crazy, I mean certifiable -- and not in a fun way like my family.

Carly and I were roommates my sophomore year in college. It was kind of a forced cohabitation on both our parts. Neither one of us liked one another, but space was an issue in the dorm we both wanted to live in. We compromised and all the animosity turned into an enduring friendship one drunken night over a shared can of beets (long story).

We were pretty much inseparable -- and incorrigible -- from that moment on.

We spent three hazy years nursing hangovers, bullying additional roommates and mocking the multitude of men that moved throughout our lives (and beds). She ultimately found one that she liked enough to commit to -- and they moved in together right after college.

Her betrothed, Kyle, was a likable guy with a fun personality and an easygoing nature. In fact, he was so engaging I was sure he was gay for the first year of their relationship. I don't think it helped his cause that he held a cigarette between his middle and ring finger and once wore a "God made Adam and Steve" shirt. We found out, after the fact, that he did it as part of a dare from one of his roommates.

Kyle's easygoing personality was a must if he was going to marry Carly, though. I love her to death but the girl is high maintenance. She's one of those people that always has a "to do" list -- and actually gets it done every day. I'm one of those people who has a "to do" list and hopes to get it done someday. Heck, I'd be happy if I got one or two things done on it before I die.

Carly's parents live in Chesterfield Township, a northern suburb of Macomb County and a good twenty-minute drive from my house. She was currently back living with them as a concession to her mother for living in sin with Kyle for the past few years. Carly said it was easier to acquiesce to her mother's demands for purity than argue with her. Of course, her mother must have been a moron to think Carly was spending all those nights "planning her wedding" at my house. Three nights a week. Three nights a week that I never actually saw her, but on which she always called me to remind me to lie to her mother should she call.

For my part, I had no problem lying to Carly's mom. My mother is a different story. First of all, she would never have believed a lie like that. Of course, I never would have lied about something so mundane anyway. Watching my mother's head spin around like that kid in *The Exorcist* when I told her I was going to fornicate with someone held more appeal for me than lying anyway.

When I got to the house, I realized right away something was off. Carly's mom was sitting on the front steps crying. I noticed her lips seemed to be moving, but there was no cell phone to her ear.

Odd, but not unexpected. I figured whatever was going on here had been propelled by a few drinks. Oh, and when I say a few drinks, I actually mean at least fifteen.

"Hey Mrs. Starling," I greeted her amiably as I swung out of the car. She didn't appear to notice me. Instead she continued her running commentary while resting her head against a ceramic goose dressed in a Detroit Red Wings jersey that sat on the front stoop.

"I told her, I told her that if she gave away the milk for free, then no one would buy the cow."

I looked around the yard in case I just wasn't seeing whomever she was talking to. There was no one there.

"Now what's she going to do? She gave away her virtue and you can only pop that cherry once."

Yikes. Too much information.

I slid past Mrs. Starling and let myself into the house. I'd been there enough times to be considered auxiliary family. In my family, I'd be considered one of the Munsters. Someone who fit right in to an admittedly already weird clan. In the case of Carly's family, I was like Marilyn Munster -- but family all the same.

I walked into the kitchen and found Carly calmly sitting down at the kitchen table and shredding paper.

"What's going on?"

She didn't answer immediately. I saw that her shoulder length brown hair looked like it hadn't been washed yet today -- something that was very unlike Carly. I also noticed her eyes were red-rimmed -- and not from doing something fun.

"What's wrong?"

Carly turned and regarded me stonily (again, not in a fun way). "The wedding is off." She was matter-of-fact. Hmm, I must have missed the theatrics and histrionics. Or they were still coming. That was a sobering thought.

"The wedding is off? Again?" I couldn't get too concerned. Carly had called off the wedding five times in the last year. I doubted it would last. "It was on when I called you an hour ago."

Carly gave me a withering look. If I was anyone else I'd be scared. Since I was me, though, I was merely perplexed.

"Kyle's mother is in town." Carly's affect was pretty flat. If this was *Invasion of the Body Snatchers* I'd be worried.

"You called off the wedding because his mom came to visit?" I was really only half listening. I figured Carly would vent and then get over it like she always did. I reached into the donut box on the table and pulled out my favorite, a cake donut with chocolate icing and sprinkles. Yum.

Carly glared at me. "You have met his mother right?"

I had actually met his mother and found her to be just about the biggest bitch in the world. She lived in Chicago, though. I figured, at most, Carly would have to see her twice a year and once they were married Carly could be as bitchy as she wanted right back, so I didn't see the hassle. In the end, Carly was going to outlive the old biddy anyway, so she had a built in victory already.

"Yeah, I met her. She's a hag. So what?"

Carly sighed. She already had that patented disappointed mother sigh down -- and she wasn't even my mother. "So, she came to town for three reasons. First, she asked Kyle if he really wanted to marry me because she thought he could do better."

"Stupid bitch," I nodded sympathetically. I may not get the urge to marry, but I'm loyal to a fault. If Carly wanted to go beat the shit out of her future stepmother right now, I'd carry the bat for her.

"He told her he loved me and wanted to marry me."

I nodded approvingly. Kyle was loyal, too. That's one of the things I loved about him.

"Then she informed him she picked out a dress for the wedding," Carly rattled on, clearly battling to hold her emotions in check.

"What's wrong with it? Is it tacky? Is it sequined?"

Carly shook her head angrily. "It's off-white."

Now I was confused. "Well, is it like see-through or something?"

Carly clenched her jaw, clearly fighting the urge to beat me with a bat. "No, it's just that no one is supposed to wear white at a wedding except for the bride. She's trying to steal my thunder."

Personally, I'd be more upset if someone was trying to steal my car or something, but I let her continue.

"She doesn't even want me to have my day. She wants to make everything about her." Now Carly's bottom lip was quivering. Uh-oh. Carly was quick to throw a tantrum. I understood that. Heck, I was the same way. Tears were another story, though. Neither of us did tears.

I was at a crossroads here, not sure what to do. Is this a hugging moment or a swearing an oath to kill moment? I decided to wait and see if there was more. Unfortunately, there was.

"That's not even the worst part, though," Carly wailed, suddenly losing her battle to hold off the tears. Now I was frozen in abject terror. The sight of Carly crying was just too much for me. "You know how they have the daddy-daughter dance at the wedding?"

I nodded while awkwardly reaching over to pat her on the hand reassuringly.

"Well she wants a mother-son dance, too," Carly spat out. "And she's already picked a song. Do you want to know what it is?"

Probably not.

"It's that song from *Titanic*. The one about love going on after death. She's picked a song that suggests he's going down with the ship -- and I'm that ship!"

To me, this wasn't a life or death situation, but I knew it was important to Carly so I did the only thing I knew to do. The only thing a true friend would do. "You want me to beat her up for you? Start her on fire?"

Carly grimaced.

"I could sabotage the speakers right before their dance," I offered.

Whoops, this induced eye rolling.

"Oh, wait, I've got it, you want to go egg her car tonight?"

At this, Carly stopped and lifted her eyes. She clearly liked the idea of ruining the paint job on Kyle's mom's Bentley.

While I had her intrigued I kept going. "Let's go all out. Let's vandalize the hell out of Kyle's apartment while we're at it." He clearly deserved it for not staking his mother in her sleep.

Carly smiled for the first time that day and slowly got to her feet.

"Let's go shopping."

Carly smiled and reached for her purse. When she did I got a whiff of her. She smelled as dirty as her hair looked.

"Right after you take a shower," I prodded.

Seven

If she were a lesser person, Carly would have belted me one -- or at least pulled my hair and called me a dirty skank. Because she was who she was, though, instead she thanked me for not letting her go out to vandalize private property looking anything less than her best. After all, if we did it wrong mug shots could be involved.

Before she went up to shower, I asked her about her mom -- who was still outside talking to thin air.

Carly waved off the question with a laugh. "She's talking to the goose."

"What goose?" I was momentarily flummoxed.

"That stupid one she dressed up out on the front porch."

Ah, the ceramic one. Better than talking to a weather girl, I guess.

"She's worried that if I don't marry Kyle that no one will have me because I've had so much sex," Carly said as she grabbed her robe for the shower.

"Your mom lives in the Stone Age," I lamented. "Doesn't she know that being a pro at sex makes you a catch these days?"

Carly giggled as she went into the bathroom.

Waiting for Carly to get ready is an extravaganza. She's one of those people who won't leave the house looking anything less than perfect. I'm fine leaving the house as long as my ass isn't hanging out of my shorts.

An hour and a half later she was ready to go. I noticed as we left to get into my car, that her mother was no longer talking to the duck. Instead she'd fallen asleep on the porch next to it.

"Should we wake her up and move her inside?"

Carly considered it a moment. "No. That's too much work and I don't want to sweat."

Since I wasn't up for sweating either, I carefully stepped past her mom and got into the car. We drove a few miles to the nearest Target and prepared to shop.

One would think shopping for vandalizing tools would be pretty basic. Eggs and toilet paper. Frankly, that's for amateurs, and Carly and I were anything but amateurs. I'd learned my trade from the master -- my Aunt Marnie. She'd taught my cousin Lexie and me that it was an art form from a very young age -- and you could never have enough imagination when exacting revenge by property defacement.

Our first stop (after a quick gander at the clothes -- hey, we're girls and revenge can't be everything) was in the paint department. Carly was feeling especially vindictive.

"Do you think I should get white or off-white spray paint?"

Hmm, toughie. "If I were you, I'd go with red. I know you're trying to send a message about her stealing your thunder with the dress but isn't her car like an ugly taupe color? Like puke?"

Carly nodded, while knitting her brows. "You don't think the white will stand out?"

"Not enough to make a definite impression for that stupid hag."

Ultimately, Carly agreed. "You think two cans is enough?"

I shrugged. "I'd get three just to be on the safe side. We can always save it for a later date. Someone is bound to piss us off before that stuff expires. Besides, it's buy two and get the third for free."

We are nothing if not frugal.

Our next stop was the toilet paper aisle. Now this is a standard for any vandalizing excursion -- however, it's not a good option if it gets wet. Plus, the two-ply and three-ply stuff just gets in the way.

"Is it supposed to rain tonight?"

Carly pondered for a second. "I don't know, but let's skip the toilet paper. That's just too high school." Yeah, because this was a sophisticated operation.

Next up was the shaving cream aisle. We both were quiet as we looked at the options. Since the invention of shaving gel things had gotten harder when trying to make sure that your shaving cream has staying power. You're better off going with a cheap men's brand.

I was struck by a sudden thought. "You know what we should do?"

Carly looked at me expectantly.

"Let's build a giant sundae on the hood of the car and use condoms as cherries."

"That sounds fun. What can we use for the sauce?" Carly is always practical.

"What will eat the paint job?" I'm always as destructive as I can be, especially when it comes to my friends and revenge in their honor.

"The eggs will do that."

"Yeah, but we're going to use the eggs on the side of the car after we use the spray paint. Let's not double dip."

We both lapsed into silence as we thought about it.

"Maybe we shouldn't be too destructive," Carly bit her lower lip.

"I didn't say destroy it. Just something that's really hard to clean up."

We lapsed into silence again.

"I know, let's get some of that colored paste the kids use these days. In like purple or something." Carly was back on her game.

"Good idea. That will be a bitch to get off."

Ultimately, once in the arts and crafts aisle, we opted to ditch the paste and instead selected copious amounts of glitter. We rationalized that it would be a lot easier to cast about while we were in a hurry.

Our last stop was the grocery section, where we bought two dozen eggs. One dozen only allowed us each six eggs to throw and three dozen was just too decadent. We were worried we'd go crazy with the power.

We were about to check out when it happened -- the worst thing that can ever happen when you're about to do something ridiculously childish. We ran into one of our college roommates. The one we'd purposely stopped talking to because she was not only no fun -- but she was a constant downer on our fun.

Francis Talbot. Crap.

"Avery, Carly, what a surprise."

Francis' tone was clipped -- pretty much as short as her hair. She was dressed in a pink plaid suit (for shopping at Target on a Sunday, what a ponce). Her high healed shoes matched the suit to perfection (probably special order) and her once long dark hair had been shorn into one of those business cuts that equals no muss in the morning and no nookie at night, because it made her look like a guy.

"Francis," Carly greeted her in a fake saccharine voice. "Wow, long time no see."

Long time glad to not see her was more like it. I merely nodded in hello.

"So how are things ladies?" She was trying to be ingratiating. Instead she was managing to be irritating, and we'd only been around her for two minutes. Apparently she didn't want us to answer. Instead she launched into the litany that was her life. "So, I got married a few years ago and I have a son. He's a real handful. He's going to pre-school in two years and Tom (her equally lame husband) and I are going about trying to decide what pre-school to get him in. It's really the most important decision of our lives. If we send him to the wrong pre-school then he's going to be a loser in life. So, who are you married to?"

Good grief, had she finally stopped talking?

"Carly's engaged," I offered.

Carly shot me a death look.

"Oh, really," Francis enthused. "I'm so glad you finally got over that loser Kyle. So, tell me about this guy. Where did you meet him?"

"I'm marrying Kyle," Carly said through gritted teeth.

"Oh," Francis clucked sympathetically. "It's so hard to break cycles." She turned her attention to me. "What about you Avery?"

"What about me?" I knew it was stupid to engage Francis, but I figured if I didn't Carly was going to kill her.

"Are you dating anyone special?"

Did flirting with a heavily tattooed pawnshop owner count? Somehow I doubted it. Not that I'd share that with Francis anyway. "Nah, I just broke up with a guy."

"That's too bad," Francis patted my arm -- and I felt the immediate need to shower, or smack her. "Did he have commitment issues?"

"No, I did. He offered to let me move into his box with him but I didn't think it would be practical in winter. I guess that's what happens when you only date homeless guys though." I smiled widely at her. "The good part is that dental hygiene is never a problem because they usually only have a few teeth."

Francis seemed confused, not sure if I was kidding or not. Frankly, I didn't care either way what she thought about me.

What's truly funny about Francis, though, is that in college she was wilder than Carly or I ever dreamed of being. Once, at a local bar, she'd knifed the tire of a car that had blocked us in rather than wait five minutes for the driver to come out. She also once toilet papered two guys together outside a fraternity party and then lit the end of the toilet paper on fire and laughed maniacally while they panicked.

She "grew up" as soon as she left college. I personally think she just covers that crazy part of herself better than most. It's bound to come out sooner or later, though, and I didn't want to be at ground zero when she went nuclear. I did keep perusing the crime blotter for her name, though.

Francis frowned as she looked at our cart. I could tell the wheels were turning. "So, um, what are you guys shopping for?"

"Just stocking up," Carly answered brightly.

"For what?"

"Why do you care?" Yep, I'd hit my limit.

Carly silently admonished me for my rudeness with a dirty look. I pretended I didn't notice.

Francis pursed her lips. "God, Avery, just as rude as ever, huh?"

"Better than being crazy," I muttered.

Francis tapped her heel angrily. "What did you say?"

"You heard me."

"I am not crazy. I'm not the one shopping for some high school vandalization project. I grew up. You should try it some time."

"Come on guys." Carly is a lot more practical in public than I am.

Things pretty much deteriorated from there. Of course, they didn't have far to fall at that point. Francis made a hasty goodbye, while shooting Carly a look that said, "How can you still hang out with that maniac?"

I responded by shooting Francis the finger.

Once back in the car, with our goodies bagged in my hatchback, Carly turned to me. "Sooo, coffee? It's not going to be dark for a few hours."

Sounded good to me. Of course, I made a mental note to find out where Francis lived in case we had extra spray paint after our excursion tonight.

Eight

Carly and I opted for coffee in downtown Mount Clemens, conveniently next to Eliot's pawnshop. Given her fragile state of mind I had decided to withhold my problems from her -- so obviously I couldn't explain Eliot without explaining why I needed to buy a gun. That was a conversation I didn't want to have with anyone – let alone Carly. Besides, if she found out I had a gun she'd steal it the next time she got mad at her future mother-in-law.

As we walked into the coffee shop, I couldn't help but let my eyes drift to Eliot's storefront. He was working behind the counter and he looked just as good as he had last night. Damn. I was hoping he'd somehow gotten ugly in the intervening hours.

"Wow, look at him."

I turned to see who Carly was looking at. Unfortunately, she was looking in the same direction as I was.

"He's okay," I conceded. "If you like guys like that."

"Who doesn't?"

I tugged Carly's sleeve, redirecting her back towards the coffee shop. The last thing I needed was for Eliot to look up and see us drooling. We probably looked like puppies with our faces pressed against the window begging for people to adopt us. Unfortunately, in this case, adoption wasn't the word running through my mind.

We spent the next two ours getting loaded up on caffeine and gossiping about everything from politics to celebrity scandals. Before we knew it, darkness had descended and it was time to implement our plan.

We'd both changed our clothes at Carly's and we were now clad in solid black. Once back in the car, I shoved all my blonde hair under a black bandana. We were going to be in real trouble if the cops stopped us. We definitely looked like we were up to no good.

Kyle's apartment was a half hour away in Royal Oak. Carly had checked her voice mail and found that Kyle (like me) wasn't giving her cancellation of the wedding much due. He knew she was just venting. He told her he was going to take his mom out to dinner and then she was leaving the next morning and everything would be fine. He ended by telling her he loved her more than anything. That put Kyle off our hit list, but his mother remained.

We parked my car about three blocks out of the way and gathered our bags of goodies. Kyle's dinner should last a few hours, but just in case he came back early we didn't want him to recognize my car -- it was hard to miss with the *Star Wars* decals in the rear windows.

Kyle's apartment complex was only one level that surrounded a great pool, like three sides of a rectangle. The good news was that Kyle's unit was at the far end. An end that was unlit. As luck would have it, his mother had parked in the far dark corner so no one would park next to her precious Bentley and accidentally ding it. My guess was that a ding would be preferable to what we were about to do.

We sat the grocery bags down and surveyed our palette. As veterans of many a vandalization campaign, neither of us were nervous.

"What do you think we should do first?" Carly likes a plan of action.

"I would say the eggs, but they've been in the car for like three hours now so they are going to stink to high heaven." Hey, I can be practical, too. "I think we should save them for last. Besides, they'll make the most noise. Why don't you do the paint on the back and I'll do the sundae on the front and then we'll both do the eggs last?"

"Sounds good," Carly said, reaching into the bag for the paint. "What should I write?"

Now here was a problem. We couldn't do anything too personal that would point to us. We were built in alibis for each other, but we couldn't handle too much suspicion. I would never buckle, but Carly might if pressed too hard.

"Do something immature, like a high schooler would do," I suggested. "Write class of 2013 or something. That way they'll think it's kids and it will still ruin the paint job on the trunk."

Carly went to work on her end and I started on mine. I emptied two full cans of shaving cream in a big pile on the hood, tossed the glitter on top of it and then unwrapped the jumbo red condoms we'd bought. Oddly, they did look like cherries.

By this time, Carly had finished her paint job and came up to survey my handiwork. "Nice."

I reached into the bag, pulled out a tube of toothpaste and went to the side doors where I sprayed the toothpaste under the door handles. Just an added bonus for fun.

All that was left was the eggs. When I opened the first carton I had to hold back a gag. They'd already went rancid.

"Uh," Carly gasped. "Those are awful."

"Isn't that the point?"

We both donned knit gloves that we'd brought from home -- like I said, this wasn't our first time -- and let loose with a flurry of eggs. In the end, we were having so much fun that we used all two dozen and dissolved in a giggling fit.

"Oh, God," Carly gasped. "We are so immature."

Once we'd recovered, we diligently picked up the empty egg cartons, spray paint and shaving cream cans, and empty condom wrappers and put them back in our bags. There was no reason to litter -- or leave evidence behind. I doubted they would waste the time fingerprinting for car vandalization, but I didn't want to take any unnecessary chances.

We were making our way out of the parking lot when a pair of headlights flashed down the road coming our way.

"Shit! Hide!"

We both scrambled to the side of the road but there was nowhere to hide. Carly looked like she was about to panic. Her eyes had went wide and she looked like she was having trouble catching her breath.

I scanned the vicinity, looking for anything to hide behind. Unfortunately, the only option appeared to be the Dumpster toward the back of the building. I was moving before I really had a chance to think about it. I grabbed Carly's arm and pulled her along with me. Seeing where I was heading, Carly started to dig her heels in.

"No way. That thing is filthy."

"It's better than jail."

Carly seemed to think about that a moment. Doubt flashed in her eyes.

"Come on."

I'm like the Borg on *Star Trek*. Once I make up my mind, resistance is futile. Carly gave up fighting and dived behind the Dumpster with me, gagging at the rank smells that surrounded us.

"I'm going to have to burn this outfit."

I shushed her. The car had closed the gap between us and was slowing down. With any luck, it would be another resident and not Kyle. We'd only have to be crouched behind this Dumpster for a few minutes.

We weren't that lucky.

The car swung into the parking spot directly next to Kyle's mom's newly decorated car. The lights died and the doors opened. What came out was the shrillest voice known to man. Seriously, it could put little yapping dogs to shame.

"What happened to my car?"

"Kyle's mom," Carly mouthed to me. Yeah, like I hadn't figured that out myself. I put my finger to my lips to remind Carly to be quiet. We were going to be stuck here awhile – and it was going to be a lot harder for her than it would be for me.

I desperately wanted to peek around the corner of the Dumpster to see how Kyle and his mom were reacting -- but I didn't dare. All I could do was listen. What I heard was surprising. It was Kyle laughing.

"You think this is funny?"

Kyle was trying to stifle his chortle. "No, of course not, I was just surprised."

"You know your girlfriend did this don't you? I told you she was low class."

Carly made a move to get up and I grabbed her. She started to argue and I shot my hand over her mouth and shook my head in silent but defiant warning. If she burned me here I was going to be pissed.

"Why would Carly paint 'class of 2013' on the car?" Kyle was trying to be practical, even though I was pretty sure he knew it was us.

"She probably hired high schoolers to do it." Kyle's mom was ticked. I could hear her pacing in her clickety-clackety heels. "Paid them five bucks each and showed them her boobs or something. She's like that, you know."

Now I was pissed. We should have used paint stripper on her stupid car.

"Mom, go inside and I'll take care of this," Kyle was not laughing now. He seemed angry. Hopefully it was only with his mother and not with us.

"No, we have to call the police."

Shit. If the police came they would almost certainly find us and I didn't have the same capital with the police in Oakland County as I did in Macomb County. If I had to call in a favor to Jake to try to get us out of trouble, he wasn't going to be happy. Knowing Jake, he'd make us spend the night in jail to teach us a lesson.

"Mom, I'm not going to bother the police with this," Kyle argued. "I'll just hose it off and everything will be fine."

His mother harrumphed her way into his apartment. She wasn't happy with his decision, but for some reason she wasn't fighting it. I could only hope if she called the police, we'd have time to get away before they got here.

I listened closely. I couldn't decide if Kyle was still out by the car. Maybe he'd went inside with his mom. I was going to have to risk a peek.

I carefully angled myself to the edge of the Dumpster and was prepared to look around the corner when I noticed a pair of Reebok clad feet step into my view. Uh-oh. I was pretty sure Kyle was the only person I knew who wore Reeboks -- they had a distinct lack of cool factor.

"Evening ladies. Productive night, I see."

I debated pretending I didn't hear him, but that seemed like a stupid idea given the situation. Better to just own up to it and shame him into letting us go. I stood up, prepared to begin my argument. When I met Kyle's gaze, I noticed that his body was shaking with silent laughter.

Carly was pressed into my back. She was like a cat. It was like if she couldn't see Kyle, then he couldn't see her. I glanced at her, trying to get her to own up to what we'd done so we could make a hasty retreat. She wasn't making eye contact, though.

"This was my idea." Might as well try to help Carly.

Kyle smirked at me. "I have no doubt. My guess is, though, that it didn't take a lot of hard work to get your partner in crime here to go along with it, though."

Carly still wasn't speaking.

"That's not true," I lied earnestly. "I blackmailed her into coming. It was all my doing."

"You're nothing if not predictable, Avery."

Carly's grip on my arm was cutting off circulation. "Chill Carly, he's not mad at you. He knows I made you do it."

Carly looked like she was going to argue with me. Instead she shut up when she saw the grim set of my jaw line.

"Yeah, Carly, we all know Avery is the boss of you," Kyle supplied. "You would never do anything like this without her."

I shot Kyle a dirty look. He didn't seem to care.

"While I'd love to talk about this some more, I think you two should probably hightail it out of here," Kyle said. He was a little more serious now. "I have no doubt my mom called the cops. It's going to be a long night if I have to bail you two out of jail."

Well crap, I figured as much.

"You two should go."

I agreed. I grabbed Carly and started pulling her past Kyle. I figured they could hash our their domestic disturbance tomorrow. As she passed him, Kyle grabbed Carly's hand and squeezed it reassuringly. She smiled at him in return.

"You're going to owe me big for this tomorrow night," he said as we started to disappear into the night.

"Oh, yeah?" Carly finally spoke.

"You have no idea."

For some reason, I didn't doubt it. I slid a glance at Carly as we headed towards the car. She didn't look like she cared all that much that she was in debt to Kyle.

Nine

Sundays are my favorite day of the week for a multitude of reasons. One, I'm usually nursing my hangovers on Saturday mornings. Two, it's the best sports day of the year thanks to football and finals in tennis tournaments. And, three, it's perfectly okay to be lazy on Sundays. Of course, it's perfectly okay in my world to be lazy every day, but Sundays everyone gets to be lazy so I don't look out of place.

After Saturday's hijinks with Carly, I woke up feeling slightly embarrassed -- more for her than me. This is important to note, because the one trait I apparently wasn't born with was shame, so to feel any embarrassment at all on my part is fairly monumental.

Well, after fifteen minutes of feeling slightly embarrassed, I decided that was more than enough and opted to put it out of my mind. It was shockingly easy.

I actually went all out cooking breakfast and used the microwave to heat up a Lean Pocket to go along with my morning tomato juice.

Afterwards, I debated what to do with my afternoon. My lawn was desperately overgrown (and I'm too cheap to hire a lawn service) but ultimately I decided to read the paper and do something constructive -- shopping.

As I walked out to the front door and on to my porch, I realized something else was going to be in the cards. My front lawn was covered in toilet paper. What is this, high school? What kind of jerk vandalizes someone's yard with toilet paper? Hey, when I do it I have a reason. This was just destruction for destruction's sake.

I stood there for a minute, flabbergasted, as I took in the piles and piles of paper woven into the large elm tree on my front lawn and thrown over the railing of my front porch. Good grief.

"Looks like you made quite the impression on someone, mama."

Great, the white gangsters across the street were up and I was their morning entertainment.

"What do you want?" I asked Gangster Number One, trying to act like I wasn't embarrassed by my predicament.

"Want? I don't want anything. I was just admiring your landscaping. Better than lilac bushes and tree arbors, huh?"

Smart ass.

I chose to ignore him, telling myself I was doing it for his own welfare, but really I was doing it for my own dignity. I angrily stalked back to my detached garage and threw open the door to retrieve the large garbage can inside.

I carried the receptacle to the front yard and began removing the toilet paper from the tree, angrily cursing myself that I hadn't changed out of my Yoda slippers or *Friday the 13th* boxer shorts before starting my task. For the second day in a week I was mixing genres in public.

What made my toil even worse was the fact that the three white gangsters across the street had pulled up their plastic chairs to watch my progress -- while passing a bowl to toke on.

"Isn't it a little early for that?" Suddenly, I was the pot police.

"It's never too early for a good time."

I decided to pretend they weren't there -- which wasn't easy. There's nothing dignified about picking up toilet paper while still in your pajamas.

"I bet Luke Skywalker could just clean this up with his mind."

If you haven't noticed, I take a lot of grief for being a 27-year-old female *Star Wars* fan. Folks, just because I love *Star Wars* does not mean I live it -- at least I don't live it all the time.

It took me a good hour and a half to clean up the mess. Afterwards, I showered and got ready, opting to stay away from the *Star Wars* clothes for the day and instead donning a Detroit Red Wings Jersey and a pair of denim cut-offs. I topped the outfit off with my Nike flip-flops and a red bandana to keep my hair out of my face. I admired my reflection for a second, smiling to myself at the thought of my mother's face if she ever saw the outfit.

I'd decided to go to Partridge Creek, an outdoor mall in Clinton Township about 15 miles away, instead of the inside mall in Sterling Heights which was closer, for two reasons. First of all, Partridge Creek has an Apple Store and I'm a girl who loves gadgets. Secondly, it's also a dog mall and there's nothing better than people watching when the people are dressing up their dogs in little outfits.

As I arrived at Partridge Creek, I bypassed valet parking in favor of parking about mile out of my way. Hey, two bucks is two bucks. I could use the exercise anyway, I reminded myself, as I finished off the candy bar I'd happily found in my purse during the ride over.

Now, Partridge Creek isn't a normal mall. It's fairly upscale. It's greatest draw, though, is the middle of the mall, which is decked out with about five flat screen televisions, all tuned to sporting events and a comfy fireplace in the winter.

Despite the woes of the Lions, Detroit is a great sporting town. The Red Wings are always good, the Pistons are sometimes good and the Tigers went through two decades of crap but have rebounded nicely lately. As I passed by the television, I noticed a group of men watching the Tigers play the White Sox. This is a mall both men and women can love.

I headed straight for the Apple Store to see what new accessories they had for my iPad (the best invention ever -- of course I said that after the iPod, the Wii and the Kindle, too).

I was looking forward to a leisurely hour of shopping in the mall, then a steaming cup of cafe mocha from Starbucks and then, ultimately, watching the tail end of the Tigers game, when I ran into a hated face from my past.

Tad Ludington, aka, my college boyfriend. Or, even better, aka, the guy I faked orgasms with for two years. Seriously, Tad couldn't find the clitoris with a flashlight and a magnifying glass. Of course, I was the idiot that let him think he was doing it right for two years, simply because I thought I was in love with him.

I wasn't in love with him, mind you, I discovered that he loved himself enough for both of us.

What really annoyed me about Tad was that he broke up with me because he said that, even being so young, he could tell I'd never make a good political wife because I was immature and I dressed badly. He then proceeded to tell me that he'd become engaged to another girl already -- of course, this was a good girl who was still a virgin.

At that moment, I wanted to staple his balls to a tree. Instead, I mustered as much dignity as possible and walked away. I never turned back. Alright, I turned back and yelled, "You suck in bed"-- eliciting catcalls from his fraternity brothers.

He could have been right about the maturity thing.

Now, here he was again. The good news was, Tad hadn't seen me yet. The bad news? The Apple Store is wide open. I had two choices, I could run out and hide or face my ex head on.

Instead, I opted for a third choice; I dropped to my knees and slowly crawled towards the door. Unfortunately, this drew the attention of one of the store clerks.

"Did you drop something ma'am?"

"No," I hissed. "I'm just trying to leave the store."

"On your knees?"

"I threw out my back."

"Oh, do you need me to call a doctor?"

"No!" What was this guy, some kind of idiot? "I'm fine, I just need some fresh air."

I was almost to the door and safety when . . . "Avery?"

Crap. I'd know that obnoxious voice anywhere. I slowly got to my feet and straightened up. I took a deep breath to calm myself before I lost control and beat Tad's head into the glass door for old time's sake.

"Is your back better?"

Maybe I'd slap the clerk first. "Yes, it's better, thank you."

Tad regarded me with superior eyes -- and a receding hairline, if you really must know.

"Hello, Tad, how are you?"

"I'm good. I haven't seen you in awhile. Are you not covering the county commission anymore?" He was faking being polite. I hate that.

Ever since I met him, Tad has been interested in himself. That's what makes him a good politician. When he was doing this all in Oakland County, it was no big deal. Unfortunately, he moved to Macomb County two years ago and immediately got elected to the county commission here, which meant we crossed paths from time to time. Sadly, I was never in my car when he crossed my path, so I couldn't run him over.

"I only fill in at the commission," I responded airily, like I was really busy and he was holding me up. "I tend to try and go where the interesting stories are." Take that, you idiot.

Tad absentmindedly smoothed back his dark, greased back hair -- I think he thinks he's the Fonz -- and smiled tolerantly. "Well, none of the commissioners are jumping around naked with a gun, that's for sure."

"Well, I'd want to see that about as much as the 300-pound monster I saw the other day," I countered. God, this guy is a complete tool.

I turned to walk out the door, as if I was on a mission, when I froze. A tall, leggy blonde with a tiny waist, huge boobs and bleach blonde hair was walking in on the arm of Macomb County's finest -- Jake Farrell.

I cursed my luck -- and rampant consumerism -- as I scoured the room for a second exit. Apparently there wasn't one.

Jake smiled tensely when he saw me. It widened to a legitimate smile when he saw whom I was with. When I'd broken up with Jake right after high school, when he'd been in basic training for the Army, it had been for Tad.

He didn't have a lot of sympathy for my predicament. Of course, he hated Tad, too.

"Commissioner Ludington, I almost didn't recognize you with your new hair cut," Jake said smoothly, extending his hand to Tad.

"I didn't get a hair cut." Tad was confused.

"Huh, looks like there's less of it." Now, while I didn't want to encourage Jake I definitely liked Tad getting bitch slapped. I smiled sweetly at Tad while he scowled back at me.

"I should be going," he said stiffly. He merely nodded at Jake and I before he exited the store. I got a small amount of satisfaction as I caught him checking out his hairline in the mirrored door on the way out. Tool.

I turned my full attention to Jake -- and the walking Barbie Doll leashed to his arm.

Jake was still focused on Tad's retreating back.

"Um, I should probably go, too," I said. I really had no interest in meeting Barbie.

Jake snapped his attention back to me. "You didn't buy anything."

"I didn't see anything I couldn't live without." Of course, I never got a chance to browse because I kept running in to guys who'd seen me naked.

"Jakey, there's nothing a girl would like in here." Barbie speaks -- and she's ignorant.

"Oh, where are my manners, Candy, this is Avery Shaw," Jake recovered. "Avery is a reporter at The Monitor."

And someone you used to sleep with, you prick, but that's beside the point.

"Candy is a model. She works the boat show on the Nautical Mile. I met her last week." Sometimes I think Jake just talks to hear the sound of his own voice talk.

"Nice to meet you," I stiffly extended my hand for Candy (not much better than Barbie if you ask me -- which no one had).

Candy ignored it. In fact, she ignored me.

"Jake, I want to go to a real store," she whined like a petulant 14-year-old. Okay, a petulant 14-year-old with a massive boob job. "I want to go to Sephora. This is a guy store."

Since when are cool computers a guy thing? Apparently blue eye shadow and the faint smell of Aqua Net is much cooler.

"Well, I should probably go. I've had my fill of negative experiences for the week." I really needed to get out of here.

"Negative experiences? What happened?" Apparently Jake wasn't going anywhere.

I wasn't going to admit to my jealousy, so I unloaded with the first thing that came to mind.

"I got a threat with my paper yesterday."

What a dumb thing to tell a cop.

"What do you mean, you got a threat?"

I blew out a sigh. "It wasn't really a threat. It was just a note telling me to mind my own business or else."

"Or else what?"

"They really didn't spell that out."

He was quiet for a minute, while Candy apparently contemplated the meaning of uneven eyebrows in the mirror behind the display. Bitch.

"Listen, do you still have the note?" I nodded. "I want you to drop it off at the department. Give it to Derrick. We'll process it for fingerprints."

"That's really not necessary."

"Well, I think it is."

We were both quiet. I was pondering telling him where he could stick that note when I realized it would be quicker to just agree with him. Finally, I relented. "Fine, I'll drop it off tomorrow. Can I go now?"

"I'll walk you to your car to make sure you get there safely. Candy, why don't you go to Sephora and I'll meet you there."

The last thing I wanted to do was walk to my car with Jake. However, the pout on Candy's face was worth it. I smiled sweetly at her as I headed off to the parking lot with Jake at my side. I can be a bitch, too.

We lapsed into an uncomfortable silence as we made the long hike to my car. Finally, I couldn't take it anymore.

"Candy seems . . . nice."

"Don't be a bitch."

"How was that being a bitch?"

"Please. I heard the tone."

"What tone?"

"You know the tone."

"No, I don't know the tone."

"I'm not going to fight with you about this," Jake exploded. "You lost the right to care a long time ago."

"Oh, so we're going to do this again are we?" I hated it when he threw my own rampant stupidity in my face.

"No, we're not. I don't really want to go anywhere with you."

"Then why are you walking me to my car?"

"I'm not doing it because I care, I'm doing it because I'm the sheriff and your life has been threatened." He met my gaze and neither one of us believed that statement. "Maybe you should have your pumped up boyfriend do these things for you?"

"What pumped up boyfriend?" I knew whom he was talking about, but I wanted to hear him say it out loud.

"Kane."

"He's not my boyfriend, he's just my . . . friend." Not true, I know, but this fell in the category of lying for my benefit.

"He's a nutcase."

"He seems perfectly fine to me." Well, he did, in a perfectly dangerous sort of way.

"You have bleeding tragic taste in men," Jake sighed.

"You would know," I stuck my tongue out. Maturity is not one of my virtues.

Thankfully, we'd finally made it to my car and I was annoyed to see a ticket under the windshield. Great. Just what I needed.

"What? I didn't park in the valet area."

Jake walked up and pulled the ticket off to look at it.

"This isn't a ticket." His jaw visibly tightened.

"What is it?"

"Another threat."

Crap.

Ten

I walked over to Jake to take a look at the piece of paper in his hand. I was trying to act nonchalant, but I was actually wigged out.

It wasn't just a piece of paper. It was a photo. I moved nearer to Jake to get a closer look. Whoops, it was a photo of me in Yoda slippers, *Friday the 13th* boxer shorts and a white tank top, topped off with a purple robe while picking up toilet paper. It was from this morning. Did I mention, I had bed head in the picture and it wasn't pretty?

Now I know I shouldn't be focusing on my hair in the picture and I should be focusing on the big red X that was over me instead and the two little words in the right hand corner "just die" but it was really heinous bed head.

Jake didn't comment on it.

"This is getting serious," he said.

"It looks fine when I brush it." What can I say? I was defensive.

"What are you talking about?"

"Nothing," I quickly recovered.

Jake was contemplative for a second. "When was this taken?"

I shrugged. "Had to be this morning. I spent an hour cleaning up before I came here."

"You know this means someone is watching you, right?"

"What do you mean watching me? They just took a picture. It's no big deal."

"No big deal?" Jake looked incredulous. "They just didn't take your picture. They've left two notes, they know where you live and they obviously followed you here and know what you drive."

I hadn't really thought about that.

"Listen, I want this taken to the department right now," Jake ordered. "Derrick is on duty and he can put a rush on processing."

I wanted to argue with Jake, maybe it's just my nature, but I opted not to. I had a feeling it wasn't the right time. And, truth be told, I didn't like the idea that someone had photographed me without my knowledge this morning.

"Okay, I'll drop it off on my way home."

"Try not to touch it," Jake admonished.

"I'm not an idiot."

"All evidence to the contrary." Jake was gone then, though I noticed he turned back briefly to make sure I'd gotten into the car safely before he left. He could be a good guy when he wanted to be. It was rare, but it did happen.

I got into my car and headed for the sheriff's department, which actually wasn't far out of my way. As I drove I tried not to think about Jake and Candy in Sephora. It left me with a sick feeling in my stomach that I couldn't quite put my finger on. I was fairly certain it was jealousy, but I would never admit that out loud.

When I pulled up the sheriff's department, I parked in Jake's reserved space. After all, I knew where he was and I didn't feel like walking. I entered the main door and immediately walked up to the cop in the bulletproof glass enclosed bubble.

"Hi, I'm Avery Shaw, I'm here to see Officer Jackson."

The cop shushed me and continued to pore over his paper work, which I had a sneaking suspicion was probably all for show. Typical cops.

I pressed my face against the bubble. "Umm, Sheriff Farrell sent me here you know? I was just with him."

Still, nothing.

"Listen, I have a yeast infection and I need to get home and scratch so do you think you can do your job?"

Officer Stuck-up finally stopped what he was doing and regarded me with his full attention. I smiled and nodded. "Can you say itchy?"

The cop got on the phone, said a few short words I couldn't make out, and then turned to me. "He'll be out in a second."

I nodded and then moved to go sit down. I took in his face, and apparent worry that my supposed itchiness was catchy, but opted not to sit down, after all. It just wasn't worth it.

Within a few minutes I saw Derrick come out of the locked door and usher me in. "The sheriff called me."

I didn't say anything at first, merely handed over the picture, which I had only handled by the upper right corner, to Derrick. "I think he's over-reacting." I really didn't, but I was supposed to be tough.

"What about the gun?"

"I have to wait two more days for it."

Derrick just grunted in acknowledgement.

"Well, this will take a little while to process," he said, looking at the picture and smiling. "Nice outfit."

I ignored him.

"The hair is impressive, too. You give up grooming altogether these days?"

I continued to ignore him.

"Is there anything else?" Apparently he noticed I wasn't leaving.

"What's the deal with Jake and his Barbie Doll girlfriend." Yes, I'm shallow, I know.

Derrick smiled, clearly amused. "I wouldn't call her his girlfriend. In fact, he really only dates someone for about three months and then he moves along. He's one of those guys who will never settle down. I wouldn't worry about it."

"I'm not worried about it," I gave him a pissy look. "I was just curious. I met her at the mall and she's clearly not a MENSA candidate."

"And you are?"

"I didn't say that! Why do you twist everything I say?"

"Why do you care?"

"You're such an asshole."

We both knew I didn't mean it. Well, maybe I meant it, but it wouldn't last. I inherited my dad's temper. I anger quickly but get over it quickly, too.

"I have to go anyway," I said. "I've had enough of men for the day. I think I'm going to go home and just play video games for the rest of the afternoon."

Derrick and I said our snarky goodbyes, an exchange I was sure would be continued at the next family dinner, and I quickly exited the building. I got a dirty look from one of the deputies when he saw me pulling out of Jake's private parking spot. I pretended I didn't see him and moved on.

I was glad when I got home. Nothing sounded better to me than slipping into some yoga pants and playing *The Force Unleashed* on my Wii. I decided to have a quick lunch before anything else. I can get lost for hours when I play video games.

I rummaged through the refrigerator, decided on a Stouffer's macaroni and beef meal (my version of comfort food) and a container of creamed spinach. Yes, I know, I have eclectic food taste. I can't help it.

After lunch, I sat down on the couch to watch the last few minutes of my DVR'd *General Hospital* and accidentally fell asleep. It was a nice nap, filled with dreams of Jedi Knights liberating One-Eyed Willie's pirate ship from *The Goonies*. Guess my dreams liked to mix genres, too, what can I say?

I woke to find that it had gotten dark. That was some nap. I also noted that something felt . . . off. There was nothing obviously wrong, but I could just feel that there was something wrong. It was an icky feeling.

I slowly got up from the couch, trying to be careful to maneuver around the coffee table and not make any noise. I didn't want to turn on the outside light because it would probably scare away someone -- if there was someone even out there.

I made my way to the front window and tried to peer out without moving the blinds too much. I gasped when I saw a dark figure move across my front porch. I was frozen with fear for a second and then I got mad. I was going to have to beat the crap out of this guy.

I moved away from the window and carefully picked my way through the house and to the back door. I silently opened it and snuck to the garage. I reached inside the door and grabbed the first thing that I could get my hands on. It just happened to be a shovel. It would do.

I crept over to the far side of the house and made my way towards the front, trying to hide in the foliage. I peeked my head around to see if I could see the man -- yes, despite my women's lib, I assumed it was a man. Despite the darkness, the light from the main drag a few blocks away cast an ominous pall over the figure.

He wasn't very large, but he looked huge in the darkness. Plus, he was wearing a knit baseball cap in the middle of summer. That just screams criminal, doesn't it? I quietly crept up behind him as he was kneeling at the bottom of the steps to my front porch. I couldn't see what he was doing and I really didn't care.

I screwed up my courage, took a deep breath, and swung. The shovel made a horrific clang as it made contact and the figure dropped to the ground with both arms and legs splayed beneath him. I kind of felt nauseous.

Instead of checking on the status of the figure on the ground, I backed up and slipped to the side of the house to catch my breath.

I shakily reached into my pocket and pulled out my cell phone and hit number three on my speed dial.

Jake picked up on the third ring.

"Get over here now," I hissed, trying to keep as quiet as possible.

"Avery?"

"Yes, Avery. I know you have Caller ID, don't be stupid."

"Is this a personal call?"

I stopped for a second. Did he think this was a booty call? More importantly, was he up for that? I shook my head and returned to the problem at hand.

"I wish." Well, that was a stupid thing to say. "There was someone in front of my house so I hit him with a shovel. I think he's dead."

Jake was stunned. "Is this for real?"

"No, I thought it would be fun to give myself a heart attack."

"Why didn't you call the police?"

"What do you think you are?"

"I'm not the local police though," Jake sounded irritated.

Now I was annoyed. "Can you get some help over here for me or not?"

"I'm doing it now. Do not go near the guy. Lock yourself in your house until the police get there." Jake hung up and I could almost hear the disgust in his voice as he did.

Well, I could play that game, too. I wouldn't go in the house, just to show him. Really, I was too scared to move, so instead I just sat on the ground and hid behind the rose bush on the side of the house.

It seemed like it took forever for Roseville police to get to my house. Real time? Two minutes. I could see the swirling lights and hear footsteps as they exited vehicles and ran to the guy on the front porch.

I gathered all the energy I could muster and somehow managed to get back to my feet -- however shaky the stance was. I carefully made my way around the house and staggered right into two armed cops.

"Are you alright?"

I nodded breathlessly as I saw another cop lean over the body on the front walk.

"He's breathing."

I let out a sigh of relief.

"An ambulance is on the way."

Emboldened by the four cops on my lawn, I suddenly felt brave. I moved over to the side of the cop by the body and looked down as he illuminated the culprit.

I sucked in a breath as I recognized the guy. It was Lando Skywalker from the concert the night before. Great, I didn't really think he was a criminal mastermind. I did, however, think he was probably the toilet paper mastermind.

Well, crap.

Eleven

By the time the paramedics arrived, Lando had regained consciousness and he was pretty pissed off. He was gesticulating wildly as the paramedics strapped him down to a gurney.

"I want to press charges! That crazy woman almost killed me."

"I almost killed you!" I was incredulous. "What were you doing sneaking around my house in the middle of the night?"

"That's a pretty good question."

I looked up to see that Jake had arrived. I wasn't exactly his biggest fan at the moment, so I studiously avoided eye contact.

Lando turned to look at Jake and seemed to blanche a little at the sight of him. Despite his youth, Jake exudes confidence and is a pretty imposing sight -- when not flashing his heart melting dimples, that is.

"He was doing something at the bottom of the stairs, rooting around like a little rodent, maybe he was putting a bomb there or something." I was trying to be helpful, I really was.

Jake rolled his eyes.

One of the police officers came up holding something I couldn't quite make out in the darkness but my imagination thought I saw a blinking light and a big dial counting down to something. What can I say; I watch a lot of MacGyver.

"See, it's a bomb."

"It's a bouquet of roses."

"What?"

Jake smirked. "See, this is why you're single. You hit the men who want to date you with a shovel."

I glared at him and then turned to Lando. "What the hell?"

Lando had regained his defiance. "I don't want to date her. She's old."

"Old?"

"I was dropping off the flowers as an apology for last night."

"Old?"

"What happened last night?" Jake asked. "I'm almost afraid to hear this."

"She upset me at the concert because she wouldn't buy me a beer and then she left with that big muscles guy," Lando started to explain. "You know he's probably on steroids don't you? That means he has a small dick."

"Old?" I ignored the steroids comment.

"That doesn't explain why you were skulking around her house after dark and leaving flowers laying around," Jake challenged Lando.

Lando went on with his story. "I told my friends about her and they thought it would be a good idea to teach her a lesson. So we came over here and toilet papered her lawn. When I woke up today, I got to feeling bad about it and this was an apology."

Jake smiled benignly. "You really do attract winners."

I glared from Jake to Lando.

"Well, if you don't need anything more from me, then you can go." I was feeling embarrassed, annoyed and agitated. Never a good combination.

Jake waved at me and then turned to leave. "Yeah, I have a date to finish anyway."

Well, that was a low blow.

It took the paramedics and cops about fifteen minutes to get things together and leave. Lando had decided not to press charges and I had done the same. He was going to be taken to the hospital as a precaution. Despite his stupidity, I was glad he wasn't seriously hurt.

I glanced at my watch as the cops pulled away. It was only 10 p.m. and now I was wide-awake. After swinging an actual weapon into a real person's head, I was in no mood to swing a fake one in a video game.

I got in my car with no clear destination in mind. I ended up in downtown Mount Clemens, ostensibly to get a coffee. In reality, I was picturing Jake with Candy and I was really hoping to get a shot of testosterone of my own. The lights to Eliot's pawnshop were turned off, though. I was torn by disappointment and relief. I didn't know what I'd do in the same room with him anyway. It was a toss-up between ripping his clothes off and puking on his shoes.

All of a sudden there was a sharp rap on my window. It was Eliot, and he looked even better than the day before. He was dressed down in worn denim jeans and was wearing a black tank top that completely showed off his muscular arms -- which were tattooed all the way up, I noticed.

I rolled down the window with trepidation.

"What's going on?"

I didn't know how to answer that. I decided to lie. "I was hoping to get the gun. Tomorrow is the third day and it will be tomorrow in two hours so what's the harm?"

"The law is the law."

How could someone so cute be so annoying?

"I guess you're going to have to hang out with me until midnight." His smile was slow and seductive. That made me nervous.

"What did you have in mind?" I had a sudden case of dry mouth.

"I thought I'd get you liquored up and then take advantage of you." He was direct, you had to give him that.

I narrowed my eyes in mock disgust.

"Or, I'll just buy you a beer." He gestured to the bar across the street. I blew out a sigh. I really could use a drink.

I turned the car off, got out and turned to Eliot. "I want you to know that I'm doing this not because I want to sleep with you, but because I've had a shitty day and I really need a drink." Or ten.

Eliot just smiled and ushered me across the street.

The Vampire Lounge is kind of a dark little hole with live music. The owners had changed the name and theme numerous times -- including Barnacle Bill's when *Pirates of the Caribbean* came out. Now they were trying to take advantage of the vampire craze. Unfortunately for the owners, no one ever came to it whatever the theme. That was good for me, because I really wasn't in the mood for a lot of people.

My eyes slowly adjusted to the darkness and took in the clientele. There were a handful of hardcore regulars up at the bar and another couple fondling each other in the corner. No one I cared about either way.

Eliot made his way to a table at the center of the room and I took a seat across from him. I was trying to avoid eye contact for some reason. I really didn't understand why.

A cute little brunette waitress with ridiculously perky boobs and a flirty little smile came over to the table to take our drink orders. "Hey Eliot," she purred. "You want your usual?"

He nodded with a friendly smile. "Sure Cammie. That sounds great."

Cammie practically melted at his welcoming smile. It was sickening. "And you?" She was clearly talking to me, and yet she didn't look at me. Whatever.

"Just give me a light beer. Whatever is on tap."

"Sure," Cammie smiled at Eliot and walked away.

"You have a way with women don't you?" It wasn't really a question. Eliot answered anyway.

"I've never had any complaints," he agreed. "I could line up some recommendations for you, if you want."

I didn't. I didn't bother thanking the waitress when she brought my drink either. She didn't even know I was in the room.

"Do you need anything else, Eliot?"

He shook his head, but patted her reassuringly on the arm as she left. What a whore.

After Cammie went to pay attention to the handful of other customers, Eliot turned a thoughtful look to me. "You look like hell."

"Thank you." Not.

"I mean, you look like you've had a rough night. I don't think you could really look bad if you tried." Good thing he didn't see the bed head picture.

"I've had a rough day."

"Why don't you tell me about it."

So I did. I have no idea why. Despite the fact that Jake said he was dangerous. Despite the fact that I barely knew him. I told Eliot everything that had happened over the past few days. Something inside me inherently trusted him.

Eliot remained quiet throughout my entire story. Finally, when I was done, he leaned back in his seat and took a long pull on his beer.

"That's quite a story."

My eyes shot daggers through him. Was he calling me a liar?

"Problem is, I have a feeling that this is just an average week for you."

I didn't know how to take that. Truth was, aside from hitting Lando with a shovel, it really wasn't an odd week for me.

"I guess I'm a little high maintenance."

"Nothing wrong with that . . . as long as you're worth the effort." Good God this guy was sexy. The problem was, I am not exactly good at the flirting thing. Guys usually take it as the me acting like a spazz thing.

Instead, I downed my drink and ordered another. It tasted good. "So tell me about you?"

"What do you want to know?"

"Well, for one thing, why does Jake hate you?"

Eliot seemed to take the question in stride. "That's kind of between us."

"Hey, I'm a reporter. Being a busybody goes with the territory."

Eliot smiled. I guess I'm cute sometimes, too.

"It's really not a big deal. We just tend to do things differently, I guess. Jake is a follow the rules guy and I'm not."

"Says the guy who won't give me my gun two hours early."

Eliot pretended I didn't say anything.

"Truth be told, I respect Jake and I even like him most of the time. I just don't think he feels the same way about me."

I thought about it for a second and silently agreed, no, Jake didn't like him. And, as much as I would like to believe otherwise, it wasn't just about me. I was just a contributing factor. A small one, at that.

Eliot and I continued to drink and talk. I was surprised how easy he was to converse with. He was also quite interesting. He liked eclectic music. He loved movies. He liked video games. He was the male version of me. Or, more aptly, I was the female version of him.

When I got up to finally go to the bathroom, I realized I was drunk. I think falling into the next table was a dead giveaway – even though I tried to play it off. Eliot seemed to notice, too, as he helped me regain my rather shaky feet.

"You can't drive home."

Now, this was a pickle. I clearly was too drunk to drive home but I didn't have a lot of options here.

"You can stay at my place," Eliot offered.

Well, that was a scary proposition.

"No, I'll just sleep in my car." Was I slurring my words?

Eliot ignored my argument. Instead, he hoisted me up, threw me over his shoulder and dropped two twenties on the table. I wasn't too drunk to notice that he grunted slightly when lifting me up. That wasn't really a boost to my ego.

"Hey, you're not the boss of me!" I was definitely slurring my words. I wasn't sure, but I thought I probably wasn't cute anymore.

I didn't remember much after that, just darkness.

Twelve

I woke up to a feeling of intense pain. The light was far too bright. My mouth tasted like it was bathed in cotton. And my head legitimately felt like it was going to explode into a million little pieces. How did this happen?

Whoa, wait, where did this happen? I clearly wasn't in my own bed. That was my second thought.

"Wow, you look scary in the morning."

Crap, here was my third, I was waking up on the couch of the hottest man I'd ever seen in real life and I was hung-over as hell. I don't look great in the morning on a good day. I didn't even want to know what I looked like this morning.

"Coffee." I sounded like I had a frog in my throat -- and it was dying.

Eliot sat down on the end of the couch next to me and I saw his face for the first time this morning. He looked flawless. Despite his long hair, he apparently didn't wake up with bed head. Sometimes life just isn't fair.

I struggled to a sitting position and accepted the professionally made cafe mocha he shoved in my face. "You went to the coffee shop?"

"Yeah, I don't make my own coffee. I don't like it."

I filed that away for future reference. The beautiful in the morning man didn't like coffee.

"I guess I got a little drunk last night," I stated the obvious. "I'm really not a very good drunk."

Eliot smirked. "You were fine, if a bit heavy to carry across the street. I guess I'm glad that you didn't eat dinner before hand."

I grimaced. He clearly thought I was fat.

He must have read my mind. "You're not fat. You're solid. I like a woman with a little meat on her bones instead of someone who starves herself."

I was pretty sure I'd been insulted. Solid is code for lard butt. "I need breakfast." Hey, I couldn't change my solidity right now, and my stomach was rumbling as if it hadn't been fed in years instead of hours.

"Well, if you get up and get in the shower then I'll take you to breakfast. Then I'll get you your gun and I'll show you how to shoot it."

Right, the gun. I struggled to get up and momentarily lost my balance. Quick as a cat, Eliot grabbed my arm to steady me. "Where's your bathroom?"

Eliot pointed down the hall. I took my coffee with me. I figured I was going to need it. When I walked into the bathroom I got my first look at myself and it wasn't pretty. My hair was pasted to the side of my face and I'd clearly drooled on myself in my sleep. Nice. In addition, the little bit of mascara I'd put on the night before was now smudged halfway down my cheek. I was definitely lust worthy.

I mainlined the rest of my coffee and climbed into the shower. There was nothing I could do about it now.

Twenty minutes later I walked out of the bathroom in the same clothes from the night before, but feeling infinitely better about my appearance. I had that pink, just showered thing going for me, despite my lack of makeup. I was at least presentable again.

Eliot was sitting at his small dinette table, reading The Monitor. He looked up briefly when I walked in the room.

"I can loan you a T-shirt if you want?"

"I'm fine," I said looking down at the Red Wings jersey. It didn't look too bad to me, despite the amber stain splashed on my breast. "So, how about that breakfast?"

We went downstairs and I noticed his pawnshop was open. "How is your store open when you're here with me?"

"They're called employees."

Smart ass.

We both walked down the street to the Coney Island. The food may be unhealthy but it was delicious. Once inside, I greeted the owner with a friendly smile. I was in here a lot.

Eliot ordered pancakes while I went for eggs, hash browns, ham and toast. When in doubt, go with the grease.

We kept the conversation light over breakfast. There really isn't much to say after you pass out on a guy and he has to carry you home. You just pretend it didn't happen.

When my breakfast made it to the table, I couldn't help but dig in with gusto. I tend to eat with enthusiasm.

Eliot seemed amused at my vigorous egg dunking.

After a few minutes of nonstop eating and no talking, I noticed that Eliot's attention had been diverted to the door at the front of the diner. I almost didn't want to look, which made me have to look.

I turned around and caught sight of Jake swaggering in alone. He seemed to freeze in time when he saw us. This wasn't going to be good.

I could almost see the mental struggle engulfing him. In the end, he decided to acknowledge us rather than pretend he didn't see us.

"Avery, Kane," he said, sliding into the both across the aisle from us. He thanked the waitress as she brought him a cup of coffee and a menu.

I didn't know what to say. It was kind of an uncomfortable situation. I looked over at Eliot. He was smiling widely. He seemed to like the situation.

I decided to make the first move. "Have you heard how Lando is doing?"

Jake looked blank.

"The guy I hit with a shovel."

Jake shook his head. "The guy's name was Lando?"

"Yeah, Lando Skywalker."

Eliot barked out a loud laugh. Even Jake looked amused. "Seriously, where do you find these people?"

I ignored him as I started cutting into my slab of ham. Screw them both.

"Well, Lando is fine. He was released this morning. I don't think you have to worry about him bringing you flowers again."

Well that was good news.

Jake placed his order while I polished off my breakfast and then looked to Eliot's plate. He'd only ate half his pancakes and one of his sausage links. He saw me licking my lips and pushed the sausage plate towards me.

Jake witnessed the exchange and frowned. "Isn't that the outfit you were wearing when I saw you last night?"

Don't answer that. Divert.

"I'm getting a gun today and Eliot is showing me how to shoot it."

If Jake noticed I didn't answer his question he didn't make it obvious. Instead he shot a glare Eliot's way.

"You sold her a gun?"

"She passed the background check."

"Yeah, and she's also the most unbalanced person I know."

"It's not like I'm going to get my period and shoot someone." Geez.

Both Eliot and Jake regarded me suspiciously.

"Someone would have to really piss me off to get me to do that."

Jake raised his eyebrows.

"No, I mean really piss me off."

Both men were still silent.

"Screw you both."

Eliot merely smirked and plopped a few bills down to pay the tab. "Well, come on Hickok, let's get you armed and dangerous."

He nodded in goodbye to Jake and waited for me to get up and follow him. I got the distinct feeling that Jake was watching us leave and he wasn't happy. It gave me a perverse thrill.

After retrieving my gun, Eliot took me to the gun range in Clinton Township. I didn't know what to expect, but this wasn't it. It was filled with middle-aged white fat men. I was the only woman. I guess I knew where all the men went to get away from their wives on Sunday afternoons now. Of course, that was information I never really needed.

Eliot was eternally patient as he showed me how to load the gun and aim it. I got the feeling there was a question he wanted to ask, but didn't know how to broach. Finally, I couldn't take the tension anymore.

"What?"

"What's the deal with you and Farrell?"

Well, that's a loaded question. "What deal?"

"Don't be cute. Seriously, I can tell you have a past."

I met Eliot's gaze and knew lying wasn't really an option. "We went to high school together." Hey, omitting information isn't really lying.

Eliot arched his right eyebrow and waited for me to continue.

"We dated in high school."

He continued to wait.

"Okay, we were kind of engaged."

Eliot just took the information in and didn't react.

"Well, we weren't really engaged. It was more like we were engaged to be engaged. He gave me a promise ring."

Eliot grinned at my discomfort. "What happened?"

"What do you mean what happened? I was sixteen. He went into the Army and I went to college. We were just too young."

"And now?"

"There is no now." I mostly believed that. "We are two people who used to date who happen to run into each other all the time because our careers overlap."

After the shooting lesson, Eliot said I wasn't half bad, I decided I needed to go home and have a nap. Eliot had another idea.

"I think we should run out to Partridge Creek."

"Why?"

He looked at me like I was from another planet.

"Because that's where you were threatened yesterday and they happen to have their parking lot wired with video cameras so we could at least see if we can recognize who left the photo on your car."

Huh, why hadn't I thought of that?

"What makes you think they'll just let us watch their security videos?"

"I know the head of security." Of course he did.

I pushed the thoughts of a refreshing nap out of my head. Some things were more important. "Let's go."

When we got to the mall, Eliot went for the valet parking, which kind of surprised me. He didn't seem like the valet type of guy even though he drove an expensive Jaguar.

He caught me looking at him. "It's just quicker."

I shrugged. I didn't really care.

Eliot knew the way to the security office, so I followed. My hangover didn't allow me to take the lead. In fact, Eliot was lucky I managed to remain on my feet at all. Once inside, he greeted the guy at the desk with a friendly wave. "Hey Tom, do you think I could look at the security footage from the parking lot from yesterday?"

Tom didn't even ask why. "Sure. You know how to use the equipment right?"

Eliot nodded and headed to the back of the office and sat down at a monitor. He immediately started a search. "What time did this happen?"

I told him and he started searching through the footage. "Where did you park?"

After about five minutes Eliot navigated the footage until he found my car. I had just pulled in and the camera showed me shoving a Snickers bar into my mouth as I exited my vehicle. Hey, apparently I'm solid.

Eliot fast-forwarded the footage for about twenty minutes, until a figure appeared in the frame and moved towards my car with a purpose. We both leaned forward to get a better look. The figure was clearly on camera putting a piece of paper -- or the photograph -- under the windshield. Problem was, the figure was hidden by a white hoodie.

There were no features that were discernible. Eliot tried looking at him from different angles and there was just nothing.

"It's like trying to identify a stormtrooper," I lamented. "It's impossible."

Eliot looked at me sideways. "You really are a nerd's wet dream, aren't you?"

Thirteen

In my world, Monday mornings are ugly. To be fair, most mornings are ugly, but Mondays make me want to shoot someone. Guess it's good I now had a gun, which I'd conveniently put away in the desk drawer in the office. Out of sight, out of mind.

I was already running fifteen minutes late when I got into the shower, so to cut time I took an extra ten minutes under the soothingly hot water. I needed to wake up.

By the time I got to work, the newsroom was predominantly empty. Most copy editors work nights and all the reporters were in the weekly meeting. I silently cursed myself for being late, glanced down at my black and white plaid Capris and juniors black tee with the words "Vader was framed" on it. I knew Fish was going to be livid when he saw me, but there wasn't much I could do about it at this point.

I went into the meeting room, trying to slide into a chair without Fish noticing. It didn't really work in my favor.

"Nice of you to join us, Avery."

My co-workers just rolled their eyes. I really missed Marvin at these meetings, but he worked a later shift so he wouldn't be in for a few hours.

"Sorry, my alarm didn't go off." This was a regular excuse for me.

Fish frowned at my answer. I decided to answer the glare with my best fake smile.

"So, what were we talking about?"

Apparently that was a question I shouldn't have asked, because everyone groaned in response.

"Well, I was telling everyone about the dinner I had at El Charros."

My eyes found their way to the end of the table and took in Melvin "Ribs" Kowalski. Everyone else seemed steadfastly trying to ignore him. Melvin is a nice guy. He's a 60-year-old Polish American with a gregarious personality and a really cheap pocketbook. He's also obsessed with food. He reminds me of Dom Deluise, for some reason.

Melvin is one of those people who manages to get a free meal wherever he goes -- and it's always "tremendous." Apparently, the cheaper the meal, the better it is in Melvin's world.

Melvin continued on his food rant, purposely ignoring the look of boredom on everyone's faces. Apparently my outfit wasn't the most irritating thing in the room. "So we ordered dinner and they brought out this huge bowl of chips and salsa. I'm telling you, this was the best salsa I've ever had in my life. It was tremendous. Did you know these chips are free? Anyway, we just loaded up on the chips and took the food home to have later. That way we got two meals for the price of one."

Everyone sighed with relief because they thought Melvin was done. Boy, were we wrong.

"Then, on Saturday, we went to that new Polish place in the Clem," he barely took a breath, I swear. "You have to pay by the pound. It's one of those cafeteria-style places.

And they had these great looking ribs. So, you know what you do to save money? You cut the ribs from the bone and leave the bone on the buffet. It's cheaper and more filling."

"Isn't that stealing?" I didn't even know who asked the question, but it's the same one that went through my mind, so I looked up to Melvin to hear the answer.

"No, it's not stealing. They want you to do that. They expect it. Don't be ridiculous."

I didn't even know what to say to that. Fish apparently did.

"Maybe instead of focusing on ribs, you should focus on your writing."

While Melvin may be personally likable, professionally he's a menace. He spells everything wrong, he never fact checks and he attributes everything to "some guy". I think he's capable, but he's just lazy. He once quoted himself in a weather story, I kid you not. "It's a beautiful day today," said Melvin Kowalski.

Melvin looked unconcerned by Fish's consternation. "What are you talking about?"

"I'm talking about the story you filed on Friday?" Fish wasn't backing down. This didn't look good.

"That was a great story."

"It was tremendous." I looked around, about four of us had said it in unison under our breath, so the whole room had heard.

Now Melvin looked annoyed.

Fish just continued like he hadn't heard us. "Yeah, it was a great story. A great story that quoted the dead guy."

Whoops. Like I said, Melvin isn't exactly known for his accuracy.

"Your story, it quoted the dead guy instead of the cop." Fish was livid. Of course, my question was, why didn't the copy editors catch it, but it didn't seem like a good time to bring it up so I let it pass. I was comfortable with Fish's rage being directed at Melvin, and not at me.

Melvin seemed unimpressed with the anger. "Maybe that's what the dead guy was feeling?"

Things quickly degenerated from there and I thought I'd escape the meeting relatively unscathed until Fish threw one last line out.

"Oh, Avery, you'll have to cover the county commission meeting this afternoon. No one else is available."

Well crap.

Given Fish's mood, I decided not to argue but that didn't stop me from grumbling all the way back to my desk. When I checked the clock, I realized I'd lost a whole hour of my life to that meeting and now I'd have to lose about five more during a county commission meeting that would focus on the county's dwindling budget.

Macomb's government consists of a county board, made up of twenty-six commissioners, who all vote on what's in the best interests of their district. Recently, as a cost cutting move, the residents of the county decided to switch over to a county executive form of government. When this goes into effect in six months, half the commissioners are going to lose their jobs and now they're all jockeying for political position -- including my ex-asshole Tad.

After typing in a few briefs and obits, I made my way downtown, parking strategically in front of Eliot's pawnshop instead of the courthouse and walked the three blocks down the street. I think I was secretly hoping to run into him. I didn't. There was some pretty young girl working the counter when I walked by. I mentally cursed myself for caring.

By the time I got to the county building a few blocks down, I noticed a large crowd picketing on the sidewalk in front of the modern looking monstrosity. I noticed our photographer, Jared Jackson, was happily snapping pictures of one big-busted picketer -- while glancing sideways at a well-muscled male one in tight jeans. Good grief.

I walked up to a middle-aged man with brown hair that was graying at the temples who was hanging around the outskirts of the crowd. "What's going on?"

When the man turned to me, I noticed his shirt for the first time and couldn't help but smile. It was one of those screen-printed deals with a picture of the head of the commission, Clara Black, dressed in Nazi regalia. You have to love small town politics. People go nuts -- but it makes my job so much easier.

"We're protesting water rates." The man said it to me like I was an idiot. His attitude apparently stemmed from the fact that I didn't just know what the problem was.

I know it sounds boring, but water rates are actually a huge deal in the suburbs of Detroit. Essentially, the city government of Detroit controls the water rates for the entire region. With everyone fleeing the city, to balance their budget, Detroit consistently raises water rates to the suburbs. The suburbs, of course, balk at this but don't hesitate to pass the increase on to the residents. It has actually turned into a race war between the city and the suburbs, with the black residents of Detroit screaming "white flight" and the mostly white residents of the suburbs calling Detroit crooked and lazy. In my opinion, they both had a point.

"Are they raising rates again?" I don't cover county politics very often, so I had to catch up.

The guy looked at me like I was an alien.

"So, how big of a increase are they proposing?"

"Five percent."

That's actually a pretty big increase for people who are losing jobs left and right.

"That's not the only issue either," the guy said. "The infrastructure of the water department is falling into disarray and those costs get passed on to us, as well. As they continue to lay people off, that infrastructure just continues to crumble because they don't have enough people to keep it up and the whole thing is going to hell."

Great, this is going to be a long meeting.

I introduced myself to the man and asked him if I could quote him. He was eager to be in the paper -- most people are -- and he wasted no time spelling his name for me. Rob Jones wouldn't have been too hard for me to figure out on my own, though.

After getting a few more quotes, I made my way up to the seventh floor and was surprised to see that the conference area was standing room only. Great. Luckily, there was a designated media section, so I made my way over to an empty seat.

Once I got comfortable, I scanned the room. I noticed Tad in the far corner with his head bent together with two other commissioners. I noted, it was two commissioners who were usually being investigated for corruption. That didn't surprise me.

On the other side of the room, I saw Jake talking seriously with the county prosecutor, Terrence Moore. Terrence and Jake were both young politicians who were elected off the names of their deceased fathers -- and both had a chip on their shoulder because of it. Thankfully, they were both good at their jobs, even though they tended to be hot heads. At least they were both infinitely quotable.

I greeted some of the other media in my area, two from the large dailies in Detroit and one from the smaller weeklies. I ignored the three television reporters; print and broadcast just don't mix.

The meeting was as long as I'd thought it would be. Most of it was boring, but occasionally the name-calling and finger pointing was actually fairly entertaining. In response to the county proposing to cut his staff, Terrence threatened to sue the county -- which freaked everyone out.

In his own tightly controlled diatribe, Jake pulled out the old "so you want your residents to be in danger" argument. He clearly didn't want to lose any deputies. Tad started speaking down to him in response and

Terrence had to physically restrain Jake at one point to stop him from jumping over the gate to get to Tad. To me, that would have been the best story ever.

I also noticed that the commissioners were glossing over the fact that there was a discrepancy in the water budget. A discrepancy that added up to a little more than $500,000. That usually meant embezzlement.

I saw Rob Jones get up during the public participation part of the meeting and deliver a pretty well-written, if long-winded, speech. I noticed Clara's reaction when she saw the shirt and couldn't help but smirk.

Finally, the meeting broke up and I began to move around the room to gather a few last minute quotes from the politicians. Unfortunately, the first one I ran into was Tad.

"So, Mr. Ludington, how did you feel the meeting went?"

"You need to control your boyfriend."

"What boyfriend would that be?"

"Our esteemed sheriff," Tad glowered. "He seems to think he's all that and a bag of chips."

"Yeah, my great-grandmother just called, she wants her saying back."

"You're a bitch."

Before I knew what was happening, Jake had a hold of Tad's shoulder and was roughly shoving him out of my line of sight.

I was torn. On one hand, I wanted to see Tad get his face beat in. On the other, this could cost Jake his career. I didn't get a chance to decide because, before I could, a large barreled chest covered in blue flannel was pulling Jake away from Tad. It was Eliot.

"Let it go man," Eliot was trying to calm Jake down. "The guy's a douche. Let it go."

"What are you doing here?" I hadn't expected to see Eliot. Politics didn't seem to be his thing.

Eliot didn't meet my gaze. He was too busy gauging Jake to see if he was about to commit murder. "The council was worried that something might happen, so they had me wiring the room with cameras that caught every angle."

I took that information in for a minute as I watched Eliot warily let Jake go. Tad had regained his footing and was now incensed.

"I want that man arrested," he said pointing at Jake.

"For what? From my perspective you attacked him." Like I said, I can lie when it benefits me.

"What?" Tad was outraged. "You saw it!"

"I saw you attack him."

"Well, your roided up boy toy over there has it on tape."

Eliot's expression didn't change and he didn't acknowledge the steroids comment. "The camera on this side of the room isn't working. I was trying to fix it all meeting. As a witness, though, like Ms. Shaw, I saw you attack the sheriff."

Tad was dumbfounded. "Aren't you two fighting over this slut?" He was gesturing to me. "I thought that was the county gossip. Why would you possibly be taking his side?"

"Did you just call me a slut?"

"There are no sides," Eliot said smoothly. "There is only the truth and the truth is that you attacked the sheriff first and it's only out of the goodness of his heart that he's not pressing charges against you."

"Did you just call me a slut?" I was seeing red. The next thing I knew Eliot was pulling me off of Tad, who was trying to brush his receding hairline back into place.

"You're a menace," he seethed. "I want charges brought up against you, too!"

Eliot sighed. "Ms. Shaw only got involved to protect Sheriff Farrell."

Jake nodded stiffly and silently in assent. He wasn't fond of me right now, but he really hated Tad.

For his part, Tad was speechless.

"You'll all pay."

Well, almost speechless.

Fourteen

After Tad departed, the three of us were left in an uncomfortable silence. Jake was mad because he felt indebted to Eliot. Eliot was mad that he had been put in the situation to protect Tad when he'd much rather kick his ass himself. And me? I was mad that no one had beat the snot out of Tad for calling me a slut -- and that neither Jake nor Eliot seemed all that interested in me, or my woes, at the moment.

I'm shallow, I know.

Finally, Jake broke the silence.

"You didn't have to lie for me. I made the mistake. I should have taken responsibility."

Eliot shook his head in disgust. "You just can't say thank you, can you?"

"I had the situation under control."

"Yeah, clearly."

Actually, what seemed to be clear was that I was no longer important to the conversation. I didn't even bother to say goodbye. Instead I made my way across the room to Clara Black to get her take on the meeting.

"I'm actually running late," she said tersely. "You can ride down in the elevator with me to get a quote, but that's all the time I can spare."

Beggars can't be choosers.

The ride down to the first floor was pretty tense. Black was clearly agitated by the meeting -- and the fact that anyone would dare call her leadership into question. I was annoyed that neither Jake nor Eliot had noticed me leave.

"So, do you think the missing money has been embezzled by someone in the department or on the commission?"

"Ms. Shaw, Macomb County has an extremely large budget," Clara responded, clearly annoyed by my question. "I'm sure once we have a forensic accountant conduct an audit we'll find that that money has been funneled to another department."

"You're saying you lost it?"

"No, I'm saying it's just been . . . misplaced."

"Well, I'm no genius, but I think misplaced and lost mean the same thing."

Clara didn't respond.

"From a political standpoint, is it really better to lose it than to have it embezzled?" I was genuinely curious on this point.

"It hasn't been embezzled. It's just been shuttled to a different department. We just have to find it."

As the elevator neared the bottom of the steps I decided to let my attitude do the asking and really go for broke.

"So, what do you think your chances are of retaining a seat when the districts are redrawn? I mean, you're not particularly well liked right now."

Clara looked incredulous and opened her mouth to deliver what I was sure was going to be a first rate diatribe. She never got the chance. When the doors to the elevator were opened, we were both doused with a bucketful of water.

I stood there in shocked disbelief, while Clara flew into a tantrum.

"What the hell are you doing?"

I noticed Rob Jones sitting on the other side of the door looking unapologetic. The woman standing next to him looked slightly abashed.

"Sorry," she said to me. "We thought Black would be alone."

I still hadn't moved, but I was sure my hair -- which had been perfectly flat ironed this morning -- was now a wavy mess. Dammit.

"And why were you throwing water?"

"As a political statement."

"A political statement about what?"

"County waste. We feel that there are plenty of places to cut that won't include the water department or public safety."

"Like what?"

"What about the commissioners salaries?"

Good point.

"Rob says that before he was laid off from the water department he had a whole list of suggestions for Commissioner Black and she just ignored him," the girl continued earnestly. I could tell right away she was one of those young, idealistic individuals who would only realize the futility of it all when she got a little more jaded.

"He used to work for the water department, too?" I was distracted with trying to comb out my snarled hair, but was passively listening.

"Yeah, he handled payroll."

"When was he laid off?"

"About six months ago."

"Hmm."

"I really am sorry." The woman seemed genuinely contrite.

"I think you should bring your list of problems to Commissioner Ludington in person. Approach him the same way you did Black."

The girl smiled happily. "You think that will work?"

"Definitely." My lack of maturity really knows no bounds sometimes. I can't help it if I'm petty – or that Tad deserved it.

I decided to go back to the office despite my dampness. It was closer and once I filed my story I would be free for the rest of the day. As I made my way to my car I noticed Clara Black was still fighting with Rob Jones, but the argument had moved to a corner and the two seemed to be talking in much lower voices. When I turned to my right, I saw Eliot and Jake exit from the stairwell and they seemed to be talking to one another without throwing punches. It didn't seem friendly, but it didn't seem overtly hostile either. Any progress is good, I guess.

When they caught sight of me, they both started laughing.

"I got caught up in a political protest against Black," I offered.

"Better than an intergalactic war, I guess," Eliot laughed.

Everyone has a *Star Wars* joke.

I quickly said goodbye to Jake and Eliot, both of whom watched me leave. Of course, now I looked like crap so it was the last thing I wanted. It wasn't until I got to my car that I realized that my mostly white pants were clinging to my body and, like an idiot, I was wearing a bright pink thong that was now visible through the back of my pants -- as were my ass cheeks. Great.

Back at the office, all the gathered reporters took one look at me and thought it best to avoid the situation. All except Marvin, who was dealing with his own problem.

"So I went to the doctor," he said matter-of-factly.

"What did he say?" I was mostly disinterested. Marvin was always going to the doctor for some malady or the other. Most of them he made up in his head.

"Well, you know when I got frostbite in January from walking my mom's dog without gloves when it was 30-degrees out?" I didn't, but I nodded anyway. It sounded vaguely familiar. "Well, I've been having trouble with my fingers ever since."

"Are you sure it's not arthritis?"

"No, it's not arthritis. Haven't you ever heard, frostbite in January then amputation in July?" I hadn't. I don't think anyone had. "Well, the doctor says I'm making it up."

I had to side with the doctor on this one. I'd been through so many illnesses with Marvin I was only waiting for him to contract cervical cancer.

"So why are you in a good mood if the doctor says you're making it up?"

"He thinks I should see a shrink."

Uh-oh.

"What do you think?"

"Maybe I have a brain tumor."

Of course he did.

"I do use my cell phone a lot."

I sighed. "Is there another story on the wire about cell phones causing brain cancer?" This was the third brain tumor Marvin thought he had in the past year. They usually popped up after a science story on the AP Wire pointing out a link between cell phone use and brain tumors. He'd also gotten SARS and swine flu after those stories broke.

Marvin wasn't chastened by my question. "One day I'm going to be really sick and you're going to feel really bad."

"Have you ever heard of a self-fulfilling prophecy?"

Marvin ignored my question. "Why are you all wet? Is it raining?"

"No, I got caught in a political debate."

I pulled my damp notebook out of my pocket and put it in front of the small fan on my desk. It would take at least twenty minutes for the notes to dry. I guess I had time to catch up on newsroom gossip.

I made my way to Erin's desk -- stopping quickly at Fish's to tell him about the meeting. Luckily, Erin and Fish's desks face one another. "What happened to you?" Erin seemed concerned.

Fish didn't even blink an eye. Apparently he didn't notice any difference.

I told Erin about the political picket as Fish went into the afternoon budget meeting. I was relieved to see him go.

"So, did Melvin get in any more trouble after I left?"

Erin explained that Melvin had managed to weasel out of trouble by bringing stuffed cabbage to Fish for lunch. As usual, all problems in Melvin's world could be solved by food.

Unfortunately, the same couldn't be said for my world.

"No work to do again?"

I silently cursed the arrival of Duncan Marlow, who was carrying a proof sheet of tomorrow's features section in his hand. I noticed, without really caring, that the majority of the section front was taken up with Marlow's extreme sports column.

Despite being a copy editor, Marlow fancied himself a good writer. He had conned Fish into writing a monthly column detailing his attempts at extreme sports in the county. The problem was, after skydiving and bungee jumping, there were no real extreme sports in Macomb County.

Apparently this week's column was about go-kart racing. Wow, real life-threatening stuff there.

Duncan saw me looking at the proof and handed it to me. "Look how nice it turned out."

Despite pretending he has an over-abundance of confidence, Duncan is one of those people that actually lacks confidence. He takes his columns around the newsroom to anyone that he finds and asks them to read them – while he sits and watches you expectantly. He then expects you to fawn all over him and pretend it's the best thing ever written. Behind his back, of course, we'd all dubbed the sports column his Extreme Ego column.

I took the proof in my hand and grimaced as I read. Apparently, Duncan was the quickest person in the history of mankind to catch on to riding go-karts. The instructor told him this -- at least that's what the column said.

"Isn't riding go-karts something that seven-year-olds do?"

Duncan looked angry. Of course, he usually looks like he's sitting on a big stick, so this was an improvement.

"These are adult off-road vehicles," he said. "They aren't go-karts."

"They look like go-karts." I froze as I read further down into the article. Per usual, Duncan had made the whole thing about himself. But a certain sentence had caught my eye. I read it out loud. "The instructor commented that only someone with supreme athletic ability could catch on as fast as I did. Of course, the name Duncan means brown fighter, so I always knew I was a soldier in the world of off-roading."

Erin stifled back a giggle as she caught the disbelief in my eyes.

Duncan was nonplussed. "It's the truth. I'm a road warrior."

"Brown fighter? Isn't that really like a constipated turd?"

Duncan grabbed the proof from me and stalked back to his desk. I could hear him mumbling something about the spawn of Satan.

After catching up on some mindless chatter with Erin, I found out that one of our co-workers apparently tried to screw one of the ad-reps in a very uncomfortable position -- and I don't mean in the back of a Volvo. I returned to my desk to file my story.

Since the meeting had gone so long, my story was longer than usual and it was after 5 p.m. before I finally left the office. I had completely dried off by the time I got to my car, but the only thing I was looking forward to was a long hot bath and a few hours playing *Star Wars Lego* on my Wii.

Instead, I heated up a can of soup, turned on the television and fell asleep while watching Chelsea Handler bash Beyonce. Apparently, the Force was not with me today. I blamed it on being Monday.

Fifteen

I got to sleep in on Tuesday morning since I was covering a night meeting in Roseville. It was a nice clear day and I opted to be productive. I was going to mow the lawn, go to the gym and clean the house. Ultimately, I mowed the lawn and came in to have my breakfast while watching the women of *The View*. When it was over, I thanked the Force that my name wasn't Sherri Shepherd and debated what to do with the afternoon.

As always, laziness made my decision and I decided to take a book and lounge at Metro Beach. I showered, changed into comfortable cutoffs and my favorite tank top, which featured the face of the Incredible Hulk and the words "You wouldn't like me when I'm angry."

In an effort to dress better for work, I tossed a clean *Jaws* T-shirt and my yellow Converse in the back seat to change into later and headed for the beach. Once there, I did my usual routine of people watching -- there's something enjoyable about seeing a 200-pound woman roller skate in a tube top -- and then settled in a nice spot in the sun to read the new Charlaine Harris book. I love vampire smut.

I'd been happily ensconced in Bon Temps for about an hour when someone stepped into my direct sun. I had no intention of talking to anyone that day, so I pretended I didn't notice. The shadow, however, wasn't going away.

Instead, a hand reached down and grabbed the book from me. I looked up to see Eliot flipping through it. He stopped at a hot sex scene, read a few paragraphs out loud, and then raised his eyebrows in a suggestive manner. "Have you ever thought of actually doing it instead of reading about it?"

"I do it all the time," I huffed getting to my feet. I couldn't help but notice, however, that he looked incredible in his own white tank top and green board shorts. His legs were just as muscular as his arms, I noticed. "I'm a sex machine."

I don't think he believed the lie. He handed the book back to me and took in my outfit. He seemed to like the shorts and the itty-bitty tank top. His eyes lingered on my cleavage for a good ten seconds before moving back up to my face.

"You don't have to work today?"

"I have to go to a meeting tonight. What about you?"

"I worked this morning and I'll close the shop tonight. I thought I'd enjoy the day and take my boat out fishing."

Boat? I found myself perking up. I love boats. Of course, on my lowly reporter's salary the odds of ever affording one were pretty slim. Still, if Eliot owned one, things were looking up.

Eliot seemed to notice my interest. "You want to go for a ride?"

Of course I did. "What kind of ride?" I was trying to be cute and flirty. I think it backfired. Eliot moved in closer. So close, in fact, that I couldn't breathe. "Any kind of ride you want."

I stumbled back, almost falling over the *Star Wars* sleeping bag I'd laid on the ground. "A boat ride sounds great." Did I mention I'm the worst flirter known to man?

Eliot was amused. Apparently my ineptitude is funny.

He led me down to the boat basin, where three vessels were docked. All were huge monstrosities. He walked down to the far boat -- the Caped Crusader I noticed, ah, a *Batman* fan -- and held out his hand to help me aboard. This wasn't a boat, it was a yacht. I tried not to act too impressed.

"The pawn business must be better than I thought."

"Actually, a guy pawned this and never came back to get it. Now it's mine. I thought I'd take it out for a spin."

I licked my lips nervously. Eliot seemed interested in the movement and moved closer to me. Uh-oh.

I needn't have worried. He leaned in to reach around me and, for a second, I thought he was going to kiss me, and then realized he was untying the boat. Damn, thwarted again. He seemed to notice my disappointment.

"We could stay docked and I could show you the cabin instead, if you want?"

I narrowed my eyes dangerously. "I don't know what you're talking about."

Eliot merely smiled knowingly and handed me a life jacket. I personally didn't think I needed it. He disagreed. "The water could get choppy and I'd feel better. We wouldn't want anything to happen to you."

I begrudgingly fastened the life jacket and sat down next to the pilot's chair as Eliot maneuvered us out into the channel. If you've never been on a boat in the open water it's hard to describe the feeling of the wind whipping through your hair. It's kind of a sexy feeling.

Eliot clearly liked to go fast -- that both exhilarated me and terrified me. I had a feeling he was that way in his personal life, too.

After about a half an hour, Eliot let off on the speed and stopped the boat. We had a clear view of Canada on one side and Harsen's Island in St. Clair County on the other. It was beautiful.

"So, what do you think, is it a keeper?"

I looked up at Eliot in surprise. "Is what a keeper?"

"The boat."

"I thought you said the boat was yours?"

"It is," he answered amiably. "I just wasn't sure if I was going to keep it long-term or sell it. Given the way it runs, I'm leaning towards keeping it."

I merely nodded. I know I'd keep it.

Eliot seemed relaxed as he leaned back his handsome face, which was sporting a little bit of stubble I noticed, and soaked up the rays.

Finally, he must have noticed me staring. "Yes?"

I chewed my lip. I was feeling nosy but wasn't so sure how involved in Eliot's life I truly wanted to get. Ultimately, nosiness won out.

"Why did you come to Jake's rescue yesterday?"

Eliot seemed to consider his answer before responding. "I told you. I like Jake and I wouldn't want to seem him lose his job over something as trivial as beating the snot out of that little ferret."

I agreed.

"Did you two make up?"

"We're not middle school girls," Eliot answered. "We don't make up. We have an understanding."

"What's the understanding?"

"You ask a lot of questions."

"It's my job. Seriously, what's the understanding?"

Eliot looked away from me for a moment, taking in the Canadian shoreline. "We both agreed that neither one of us is going anywhere and that we both think Ludington is an asshole."

"That's it?"

"That's it."

"Guys are weird," I was thinking aloud. "If you two were girls, there would have been some hair pulling involved."

"You pulled a lot of hair in your day? You seem like more of a biter to me."

That sounded sexy coming out of Eliot's mouth. Unfortunately, I didn't think getting sexy with Eliot was in my best interests.

"I'm just saying that girls typically fight it out more . . . aggressively."

"I don't think of you as a typical girl." Well, that was disconcerting. "I think of you as a nerdy guy with a vagina."

"What is that supposed to mean?"

"You don't think like a girl. You're all in to *Star Wars* and video games. You don't act like a girl. You're not looking for someone to rescue you and take care of you. Hell, you don't dress like a normal girl. I've never seen you in heels and, quite frankly, I've only seen you in shirts a guy would wear."

I looked down at my itty-bitty tank top. What guy would wear this?

"Just because I think for myself doesn't mean I'm not a girl." I was getting a little angry.

"I didn't say you weren't a girl. I said I just didn't think of you as a typical girl. That's not a bad thing." Eliot smiled and leaned closer to me. This time I didn't imagine the kiss, it was actually happening. It was quick and sweet but oh, so hot. "Actually," he said in a husky voice. "I think it's a very good thing. I've never met a normal girl who held my interest for more than one night."

I think my face was on fire, and I had an incredible urge to strip right there. I don't know what stopped me. Oh yeah, it was Eliot.

He pulled away and merely smiled. "What time is your meeting?"

My what? Oh, yeah, my meeting. "It's at seven." I can't
believe I actually managed to form words.

"We'd better get going then," Eliot said simply.

I nodded in agreement, only I didn't know what I was
agreeing to.

Eliot started up the boat and headed for home. Luckily
for me the engine was too loud for us to talk over and I
had plenty of time with my thoughts. My very confused
thoughts. In fact, I was so caught up in my own thoughts
I didn't notice the swirling police lights behind us until I
saw Eliot cursing out of the corner of my eye and pulling
back on the throttle.

"What is it?"

"Border patrol." Eliot looked grim.

"Our border patrol?"

"Yeah."

"Well, that's no problem, we'll just tell them who we
are."

"We're in Canadian waters." Eliot was simple and to the
point sometimes. This wasn't a good situation, we both
knew that. In these times of terrorism, slipping into
Canadian seas was akin to beating puppies. Crap.

The border patrol boat eased up alongside us, and the
officers on board didn't look happy. Unfortunately, I
don't know any border patrol cops, so I didn't have any
favors to cash in to get Eliot out of this.

"What seems to be the problem officer?" My voice was sugary sweet and Eliot seemed surprised to hear it come from my usually acerbic mouth.

Officer number one, sporting a Fu Manchu mustache (what is it with cops and porn mustaches?), didn't seem to be affected by my faux niceness. "Did you know you were traveling in international waters?"

"No officer, we must have just gotten turned around." I sounded like an incredibly innocent and breathy high schooler.

Eliot appeared amused.

Fu Manchu asked for our IDs and we both handed them over. He studied them a moment and I was sure he was about to send us on our way with a warning. I was wrong.

"We're going to board and seize your vessel," he said succinctly. "It's very likely you're going to be facing some federal charges."

Well shit.

Eliot remained silent. That, however, was not in my nature.

"This is ridiculous!" There was nothing sweet and nice about me now. "We just got turned around. Don't you guys have anything better to do like, oh I don't know, catching real criminals? Or, better yet, there's a Dunkin Donuts just off shore, why not visit there?"

I knew I'd gone too far. He angrily started calling in to the radio on his collar, informing whoever was on the other end that they'd have guests tonight. When he got to the part about our names, though, the other voice seemed interested.

"Did you say Avery Shaw?"

"Yes, Avery Elizabeth Shaw," Fu Manchu responded.

Then another voice came over the radio, one Eliot and I unfortunately both recognized.

"This is Sheriff Jake Farrell." He didn't sound happy. "Ms. Shaw and Mr. Kane are both working on a case for me. They probably just got turned around. I would consider it a personal favor if you would help them get to U.S. waters."

It didn't really sound like a request, but law enforcement usually covers for one another, so I wasn't surprised when Fu Manchu reluctantly let us go and escorted us back to Harrison Township.

Fu Manchu managed a thinly veiled threat about never entering international waters again before he departed. Eliot and I nodded, like we were taking the threat seriously -- even though neither of us really was.

Eliot had remained silent through much of the past hour, so when he docked the boat I was starting to get agitated with him.

"What's with the silent treatment? We just dodged a very large and real bullet." A thank you would be nice, I thought.

Eliot's answer was simple, and laced with innuendo.

"I'm just wondering how it happens that Sheriff Farrell came to your rescue? Yet again."

There were no ifs left in the equation anymore. Everything had officially become complicated.

Sixteen

After sharing an awkward goodbye, I was more than happy to get away from a morose Eliot. Part of me felt bad for him, but an even bigger part of me felt bad for myself. How did I manage to continually get myself into ridiculous situations like this?

I got my change of clothes out of the car, and went to the public bathroom to make myself look presentable. That didn't look like it was in the cards for me, though. One look at my lobster red face and windblown hair and I knew even my best *Jaws* T-shirt (I have three) was not going to improve my looks today.

I shrugged into the shirt anyway and ran my hands through my tousled hair. I couldn't wait until my face started to peel. Then my mortification would be complete.

I glanced at my Swatch and realized I was running late yet again. It seems to be a perpetual state for me. It really is a little known super power.

It took me about a half an hour to get to the meeting and was surprised to see how full the room was. This didn't look good. I had a sinking feeling I had another tedious meeting in my future. Turned out, I was right.

So what had the good citizens of Roseville so up in arms? Seems the city had rezoned a parcel of land that abutted a residential area so it could house a crematorium. Personally, I think it sounded pretty cool, but, then again, I'm a horror movie fanatic. The residents seemed to think otherwise – and they were being vocal about it.

I found an open seat, flipped open my notebook and started writing. Luckily for me, the affected neighbors weren't feeling particularly practical. In fact, they seemed downright psychotic.

A little old lady, seriously, she was less than five feet tall and her purse was bigger than she was, stood up at the podium and her argument wasn't exactly rational.

"I don't want to go out and get an ice cream and have body parts fall in to it." Well, that seemed like a legitimate concern. I mean, body parts falling from smoke stacks? It happens every Christmas right?

A few minutes later, a pinched little man with greasy hair and a huge beer gut took the podium. I noticed that his pants were dipping dangerously low on his rear and he was sporting a serious case of plumber's crack, without fixing any pipes. Nice. His argument was equally rational.

"I read in the National Enquirer that people who run crematoriums are sex perverts." I read that, too. "I don't think we need any more sex perverts in the area." I agree, the thousands already living in the city were enough. "I bet these guys just want to hump dead bodies." Well, at least dead bodies couldn't shoot them down.

After about an hour of the residents screaming at the council members, the city officials buckled to pressure and agreed to rescind the zoning. Bummer, I thought a crematorium sounded fascinating. For their part, the crematorium operators were threatening a lawsuit. I laid odds, when all was said and done, the council members would end up waffling back the other way. I'd seen it before. Money talks and angry mobs move on to another complaint relatively quickly.

I greeted the mayor and city attorney, made sure I understood the legal implications, and ultimately decided I was done for the day. Before heading for home to file the story, I reached into my purse and pulled out a quick smoke. Hey, it's been a stressful day.

Unfortunately, one of the city's gadflies recognized me and cornered me to voice his concerns about necrophilia for a good twenty minutes. By the time I finally got away from him, I realized I was pretty much alone in the parking lot.

I wasn't really worried since the fire department was just across the street and the city's police department was actually housed farther down in the parking lot. Truth be told, though, I generally don't get worried in situations like this. I actually pity the person who tries to mug me -- gun or not. I've got a lot of rage and, in a fight, the person that's the least balanced always has the upper hand. I'd lay odds that on any given day, I was crazier than any mugger.

I slowly ambled over in the direction of my car, but my nose detected the slight waft of lilacs. Yum. I darted a glance around and decided that it wouldn't harm anyone to grab a handful and take them home. With my luck, though, the cops would charge me with stealing flowers. Sometimes they just like to be jerks. I think it goes with the uniform.

Seeing none of Roseville's finest, I went over to the fence and broke off two full branches. That should be plenty. I turned and started back towards my car when I felt it. A cool sense of dread. Crap, I wasn't alone.

I turned around abruptly; expecting to find another outraged neighbor or even a creepy crematorium owner. All I saw was a lone car parked about fifty feet from my car. I guessed someone was still inside the meeting hall.

Still, I couldn't shake the feeling that I was being watched. I looked harder at the car. I couldn't be sure, but even in the dark I thought I saw a hint of movement. Was someone sitting in that car watching me?

I debated my options. The smart thing to do would probably be to get on the sidewalk, avoid the roadways, and run to the police department. Problem was, that was a really long walk and I'd just smoked a cigarette.

I opted for door number two, pretending I wasn't scared and just heading towards my car. Big mistake.

As I started to move across the parking lot, all of a sudden the car's lights flared to life at the same time whoever was in it started the engine. I just happened to be right in the car's path.

Shit.

I started to run, but I already knew it was too late. The car roared into action and started barreling towards me. At the last minute, I dived to the side, landing hard on the pavement. Even if the ground was made of marshmallows I had a feeling it would hurt. This, however, was pure torture. The funny thing was, I barely noticed at the time. I jerked around to see if I could see where the car was.

Luckily for me, the driver seemed to realize it probably wasn't a good idea to hang around with the police so close and instead tore out of the parking lot. In another stroke of luck, someone must have been watching from the police department, because three officers were racing towards me. They probably thought I'd been hit.

I took the opportunity to breath. I realized I'd been holding my breath. When I did, all the pain from hitting the ground washed over me. I noticed that both of my knees were bleeding profusely, as was my right elbow. Great. Now I looked even better. I had rug burn without the fun that was usually associated with it. I was quickly becoming a prime example of "what's wrong with this picture."

When they reached me, the cops seemed surprised by my calm. I think I was more shocked than anything else, but I answered their questions the best way I could.

"I don't know what kind of car it was," I argued. "It was dark, like black or blue, and it had four doors. That's all I can tell you."

"What model was it?"

"I didn't have time to ask."

"No guesses."

"Do I look like a mechanic?"

"This is Detroit. People know cars here."

"Well, I don't. You want me to identify a X-Wing versus a Y-Wing, I'm you're girl. Cars all look the same to me."

When the paramedics arrived, they bandaged up my arms and legs and declared me "lucky." Yeah, that's just what I felt, lucky.

I felt even luckier when I looked up and saw Jake coming my way. Crap. I took in his face as he approached, noted the grim set of his jaw line, and realized that things were not going to get any better for me any time soon.

"Are you alright?"

"Just peachy."

Jake knelt down, took in my bandaged arm and leg, and looked at me questioningly. I couldn't quite read the emotion behind his brown eyes.

"I did this all to myself when I hit the ground. It's not a big deal."

"Someone trying to run you over in the parking lot with fifty cops only a few feet away isn't a big deal? So what's a big deal to you?"

"I hear George Lucas is planning a live action *Star Wars* television show." I was aiming for cute; I think it was coming off as deranged.

"Well, at least your priorities are straight." Jake turned away from me and walked a few feet over to talk to the cops. They had their heads bent close together and I couldn't hear what they were saying. Truth was, I didn't really care.

That's when I noticed another familiar figure detach from the crowd that was mingling over to my left. Where had they come from anyway? It was Eliot. Apparently he'd gotten over his anger from this afternoon.

"You look like crap."

Apparently not.

"Thanks. That's always nice to hear."

Eliot didn't appear amused. "This is serious."

"So I've heard."

Eliot shook his head in disbelief. "You really are unbelievable. Why didn't you shoot at the car?"

"Because I left my gun at home."

"Good plan."

"Hey, I'm not just a pretty face."

Jake had noticed that Eliot had arrived and he didn't look pleased. He sidled over to the two of us.

"How did you know she was in trouble? Did she call you?"

"No, I heard it on the police scanner."

Jake merely nodded. "So, what do you think?" He was asking Eliot, not me.

"I think she's a walking disaster."

Wow, I was just a compliment magnet tonight. "You know I'm sitting right here?"

They both ignored me.

"Whoever she's pissed off, they mean business. This just isn't her usual charming personality ticking someone off." Jake was dead serious.

"I looked over the security feed at the mall and whoever left her the note hid his identity." Wait a second, were these two working together all of a sudden? What's that about?

"Maybe I should have let border patrol take you two in. Then I'd at least know she wasn't in danger -- at least from anyone other than herself."

This actually brought a smile to Eliot's face. "Thanks for that, by the way. It wasn't really necessary."

"I figured I owed you from the meeting." Men are strange creatures. It seemed that any animosity between the two of them had melted away. If it were me, I'd have been pulling some hair. Or at least fake coughing the word "whore" under my breath into my hand, all the while pretending to be friendly.

"So what do we do now?"

Jake seemed to think over the question. "I guess I could assign a deputy to stay with her."

Yeah, that sounded great, a cop baby-sitter. No way was that going to happen. "Has anyone considered asking the victim what she thinks?"

"No."

"Well, I don't want a police escort. I'm perfectly fine."

"Sweetheart, you're pretty far from fine." This is why Jake and I would have never worked out. He treated me like a child.

"Well, guess what? I don't need either one of you telling me how to live my life. I'm perfectly capable of doing it myself." All present evidence to the contrary.

"Avery, I've known you since you were a kid," Jake argued. "You're the idiot in the horror movie that goes upstairs to check out the noise. You're the moron who goes into a dark alley alone when a serial killer is on the loose."

"Well that's just . . . unpleasant," I snapped back. "Last time I checked I've managed to take care of myself for the past twenty-seven years. I don't need either of you big strong men to protect me. I'll protect me."

Jake sighed in defeat. "You'll be careful?"

"Of course."

Dry that lie out and you could fertilize the lawn. I think all three of us were thinking it.

Seventeen

By the time I got home, all I really wanted to do was take a bath and go to bed. I noticed Eliot had followed me to the house and waited outside until I was safely in. It was a sweet gesture, but I was feeling anything but sweet.

I haphazardly waved goodbye and then locked the door behind me. Once I saw him drive away, I blew out a sigh of relief and headed straight for the couch. I turned on a rerun of *Lost* and let the castaways' problems take my mind off things for an hour before turning on the local news. Roseville's crematorium story was third in the night's lineup. Luckily, my little problem after the meeting had gone unnoticed. There's nothing a reporter hates more than becoming the news.

I didn't think I'd fall asleep that night. Strangely, it happened before the weather report even hit the screen.

When I woke up on the couch the next morning I was unbelievably sore. It wasn't just my injuries from the fall, I realized. My sunburn was ridiculously painful, too. Ugh.

I took a cold shower, had my breakfast and headed off to work. It didn't even occur to me to call in sick. I was saving my sick days for when I had something fun to do. When I arrived at the office, I kind of wished I had called in sick. Instead, I had to work on a city budget story. There really is nothing worse.

I'd managed to make it through the bulk of the morning without having to talk to any of my co-workers, when the pervert in the corner stopped at my cubicle. Great. John Johnson -- his parents showed a lot creatively with that name -- clearly wanted something.

I blew out a sigh, and swung around in my chair. As usual, John was wearing pants that were clearly too short. When you can see the holes eating away in one's socks it's time add a couple of inches.

John didn't seem to notice my agitation with his presence.

"Hey Avery. I was wondering if you could do some labels for me?" It's important to note that, despite my journalistic prowess, in a male dominated field like news reporting, old schoolers still seem to think it's okay to ask women to do menial tasks. I didn't feel like playing that particular game today.

"So? Do them yourself."

"I don't know how to."

"Then I guess you're fresh out of luck."

"Is it your time of the month or something?" Ugh, that's another thing. If you ever tell these men to do something themselves, you're automatically on the rag. What a bunch of idiots.

John went dejectedly back to his desk, but I got the sinking suspicion he was still griping about me ten minutes later because he was talking to Fish and pointing. Fish seemed nonplussed.

"If she doesn't want to do your labels she doesn't have to." Fish is an okay boss. Yeah, he picks on my clothes, which is funny coming from a guy who dresses like Burt

Reynolds -- in the 1970s -- but he is almost always fair. I made a mental note to be nicer to him from now on. "She's probably on her period or something."

There went my attempt to be nicer.

I was feeling relatively good about my work situation about an hour later when I managed to file my budget story before lunch. That meant smooth sailing -- and online shopping – for the rest of the afternoon. I shouldn't have gotten so excited.

Just then, my cell phone started ringing. Caller ID said it was Jake. I debated not answering it, but I figured he'd just track me down in person if I did and I really didn't want to see him due to my imminent peeling.

"Your cousin Lexie has been arrested."

Never what you expect.

"What did she do?"

"The usual. She hid in a bush and beat a pregnant woman with an umbrella."

My cousin Lexie is actually one of my favorite cousins. She's the closest thing I have to a sister. She also makes me look downright linear at times.

"Why did she beat her up?"

"She says she deserved it for sleeping with her boyfriend."

Did I mention Lexie has tragic taste in men? She's one of those people that takes on the personality of whomever she's seeing at the time. When she was living in Miami she became Cuban. Now she spends most of her time in

Detroit, so she thinks she's black. In fact, if she had a list of life goals, number one would be to have a little black baby. What can I say? She's committed to her lifestyle choices.

"Is this girl pregnant by her boyfriend?"

"That's what I gather."

Great.

"What's she been charged with?"

"Disturbing the peace."

"Disturbing the peace? Not assault?"

"I talked to the judge."

"Do I need to bring bail money?"

"No, she's been released on her own recognizance."

"Thanks. I'll be there in a few minutes."

After disconnecting with Jake, I debated going to get lunch and leaving Lexie in jail for an hour, but ultimately decided that probably wouldn't be the nicest thing to do. After all, she hadn't beaten me with the umbrella.

The sheriff's department is only five minutes away from our office and, despite my reticence, I managed to get there in ten minutes. Jake was waiting outside. So much for hiding my sun ravaged face from him.

He didn't seem to notice.

"Listen, I want to talk to you before you take Lexie."

Uh-oh. "She's not on an ankle monitor or anything is she?" It wouldn't be the first time.

"No, it's not about her. She's a mess, but she's always been a mess. I'm talking about you."

In other words, I'm a mess, too.

"Listen, I'm fine."

"We ran the prints from the note and nothing came up in the system."

"Well, that's good right?"

"It depends on how you look at it. It's good that whoever it is, they haven't done another crime. That doesn't mean, though, that they're not about to do one."

I couldn't help but agree. "So what now?"

"Now? Now we wait. Hopefully, this guy just wanted to scare you. If he didn't, then he'll come again and hopefully we'll catch him this time."

I bit the inside of my lip as Jake absentmindedly reached over and removed a fleck of skin off the end of my nose. Nice.

After retrieving Lexie, I agreed to drive her to the bus depot -- hey, I don't drive to Detroit unless I absolutely have to. For her part, Lexie was a nonstop stream of obscenities.

"That stupid bitch thinks she can sleep with my boyfriend? She's lucky I didn't fricking kill her."

I nodded, feigning understanding. "So, she lives out here?"

"No, she lives in Detroit. Her mother lives out here. The cops know me in Detroit. I thought I could do it without anyone knowing out here."

"Good plan."

Lexie glared at me. At one glance, my 4'11" cousin isn't much of a powerhouse. Five minutes after meeting her, though, you know differently. She can be deadly if she wants to. Or just plain mean.

"Are you making fun of me? Because I don't think people who look like tomatoes should be able to make fun of anyone."

"Absolutely not."

"You better not be."

After thanking me for the ride, Lexie exited my car. As I pulled away from the bus stop I noticed that she was already flirting with one of the black brothers waiting alongside her. He looked like he was carrying, and not just a gun. Apparently her heartbreak was not to be long lived.

I debated going back to the office and instead went for coffee. If anyone needed a caffeine fix, it was me.

I noticed Eliot behind the counter at his shop. Part of me wanted him to look up, despite how bad I looked. He didn't and I wasn't desperate enough to actually walk into his store. I should have.

Instead, when I entered the coffee shop, I ran into Tad and his very pregnant wife, Maria. I think this was like their seventh kid.

Tad practically puffed up like a rabid raccoon when he saw me. Maria seemed oblivious to her husband's hostility.

"Hey, Avery." Maria is always friendly. I often wonder if it's all a cover, that she actually secretly enjoys torturing me. Truth is, though, I don't think she's that smart.

"Hey Maria. Looks like you're about to pop again."

She smiled benignly. "Yeah, it's our fifth. Hopefully, this time, I'll get a boy so we can be done."

"You can't be done stretching out your vagina until you have a boy?" Hey, I never said I was classy.

"Well, I would have been happy with just the girls, but Tad wants someone to carry on the name."

Yeah, because the name Ludington rates right up there with Kennedy. "Hopefully, if you do have a boy, he won't carry on Tad's hairline, too."

Maria giggled amiably. "Oh, I think his hairline is cute." Gag me.

"Yeah, he's like a shorter and less sexy Michael Ironside."

I could tell Tad was practically seething, but he'd decided not to acknowledge my presence. That only made me more determined.

"You could always make Tad get fixed," I offered. "I read it's a lot easier for guys to get cut than women."

That pretty much did it.

"Thank you for your concern with our reproduction, Avery, especially given no one wants to knock you up."

Tool.

Maria seemed embarrassed by the exchange. "Well, we should probably go."

Probably.

I smiled a genuine smile at Maria. I guess I decided, for this day at least, being married to Tad was punishment enough for anyone.

I took my coffee and went back outside and made my way to the small little picnic area between the buildings. Maybe the best way to cure a sunburn is more sun?

I was flipping through the Metro Times to see what music acts were playing in the area when I noticed Rob Jones coming my way. Thankfully, for me, he didn't have his bucket of water.

"Hey Rob."

He didn't seem thrilled to see me, just determined.

"Ms. Shaw."

We both sat in silence for a second. He seemed to be choosing his words and I was just wishing he'd go away.

"I read your story about the water rates."

"Yeah." I didn't really care if he liked it or not. I'm a firm believer that if you make one side happy and not the other one you're not doing your job. It's better to piss off both sides. Then you know it's fair and balanced.

"I don't think you grasp the problem." Because it was so complicated. "The county government is fleecing us."

"They're always fleecing us. That's what politicians do."

"It doesn't bother you?"

I shrugged. I think I'm generally apathetic on political issues at times.

"Well it bothers me." Clearly.

I think he was waiting for the outrage he was sure I felt on the subject. He was going to be disappointed.

"These people keep cutting and cutting staff and hiking and hiking rates. You don't think that's important?"

I shrugged, I really didn't care all that much.

"You're just like all the rest of the media aren't you?" Here we go. "You're all in cahoots with the politicians to screw the American people."

Cahoots?

I continued to ignore him. He finally caught on. "You just don't care do you?"

"Depends on what the topic is. Water rates just don't whip me into an intellectual frenzy. Now, if we're talking about whether or not it's appropriate for me to wear Ed Hardy shoes to work, especially given that Jon Gosselin, that douche, has ruined the brand, that's a topic that gets me worked up."

Rob seemed stunned by my shallowness. If he continued to show up in my stories, he'd get used to it.

Eighteen

I got home relatively early that night -- and unscathed for a change. What to do, what to do? I really wasn't in the mood for video games because I was so sore and it was hours before I could turn on the new episode of *Criminal Minds* and drool over Shemar Moore. So, I opted to do the thing that makes me most happy in the world -- no, not that but maybe after the movie -- and watch *The Empire Strikes Back.*

Now, I know many *Star Wars* purists think that *A New Hope* is the pinnacle of the original trilogy. For me, though, it's always been Empire. There's something about Yoda that turns me on, and, yes, I know he's a puppet.

I was happily munching on Wasabi peas (my favorite snack), sipping from a Diet Coke and watching Han Solo be the ultimate hero when I heard something shuffling outside the front door.

Crap, not again.

I quietly got up and muted the television. A smart person would call the police to check out the situation. We all know that's not me. Instead, I peered out the blinds and was shocked to find another face pressed against the glass looking in at me.

I yelped and fell backward on the couch, my heart pounding. My phone was in my hand and I was about to hit Jake's number when I realized I recognized the face -- and it wasn't necessarily one that filled me with terror.

I slowly got off the couch and threw open the door in anger. Lando Skywalker was standing sheepishly outside. I noticed he was wearing parachute pants and a blue cape. Guess he was getting ready to go to Bespin.

"Dude, what's your deal!"

"Sorry, I didn't mean to scare you. I saw through your window that you were watching Empire and I didn't want to disturb you until after Han was encased in carbonite." Well, that was considerate.

"That doesn't explain what you're doing here."

"Oh, um, I just wanted to apologize for the toilet paper thing and then the scaring you so you had to bash my head in thing, so I thought I'd bring you a present." He handed me a large *Star Wars* birthday bag.

I took it warily. As I glanced inside I couldn't help but be thrilled. It was the cutest stuffed Yoda I'd ever seen in my life.

Lando saw my smile. "You like him."

Do I like him? He's only the best Jedi Knight ever. "He's okay."

"Good, I was worried you were too old for stuffed toys." Never.

"Seriously, you didn't have to do this for me."

"No, it's okay. I wanted you to have him." Lando was quiet for a second. "We're all even now right? You're not going to whack me with anything?" Maybe just a rolled up newspaper. Lando reminded me of a chastised puppy for some reason.

"No, we're good."

That night, after Lando left and I'd settled down to sleep with Yoda, I couldn't help but smile. Lando really wasn't such a bad guy, despite the fact that only a complete loser would change his name to Lando.

The next morning I woke up with a smile for the first time in at least a week. I silently thanked Yoda and got ready for work. In an attempt to not infuriate my boss for a change, I put on a plain white shirt and sensible black Capris. I topped them off with my loud *Star Wars* shoes (they light up). Hey, Fish wouldn't be looking at my feet.

When I arrived at work, I was surprised to see Marvin in early.

"What's up bonehead?"

He shook his head when he saw my shoes. "Are you trying to give Fish an aneurysm?" No. Well, maybe.

"Why are you in so early?"

"I'm only working half a day. I'm going to an AA meeting tonight."

This surprised me. Marvin had the alcohol tolerance of a 100-pound woman. I mean, the guy drinks two amarettos on the rocks and he's toasted. I raised my eyebrow in a silent question.

"It's a good place to meet women."

Ah, well that explains it. Marvin is one of those guys who likes to swoop in and rescue women. If anyone needed rescuing, it was these women.

"What happened to that waitress you were seeing?" Marvin also likes women in the service industry. He's a complicated guy.

"Her husband came home."

"That's never stopped you before." Well, it hadn't.

"He was Albanian." Yikes.

"And you still have your head?"

"Barely."

Seemed reasonable enough to me. "So, what's going on?"

"I've been thinking about the guy that tried to hit you."

"What about him?" It was sweet Marvin was concerned.

"I don't think he was trying to actually hit you."

"Why?"

"I think it was probably just an Asian." Oh, he's going somewhere with this.

"An Asian?"

"Yeah, everyone knows that Asian people can't drive."

"That's an urban legend, you know."

"No it's not. I've seen it. Asian people, black people, old people and women shouldn't be allowed to drive."

"And this is because?"

"They can't."

Arguing with Marvin is pretty circular at times -- and it gets you nowhere. I decided not to point out the three accidents he'd already had this year. It would just lead to a big blow up, and I really wasn't in the mood.

"Where's Fish?"

"He's out for the day," Marvin replied. He'd already lost interest in his misogynistic driving rant. Sometimes I think he has ADD. "He left you a feature story about some woman who's losing her house, though."

Ugh. A sad sack story. Another shot to the heart.

I picked up the note that Fish had left me and grimaced. He'd already set up the interview for an hour from now. I guess he knew, if left to my own devices, I would have found just about any story -- even if I had to run someone over myself -- to avoid another tearjerker.

The woman's named was Kathy Harrison and she lived in Eastpointe. She was a single mother with two kids and she was losing her house in a week. I could only hope that the children wouldn't be home. Nothing derails an interview faster than kids.

When I arrived at the Harrison home, I noted that it was about three blocks away from where the barricaded gunman had been last week. Another rundown neighborhood on a rundown street. From the looks of the outside of the house, with its sagging front porch and falling gutters, I wasn't going to be any more comfortable on the inside of it.

Better get it over with.

I walked to the front door and knocked with a purpose. If I kept things on track I could be out of here in about forty-five minutes.

I saw the door open a crack, and a small woman with sad brown eyes and huge bags under them opened the door. This must be Kathy Harrison.

I introduced myself and the woman let me in. I took note that the few meager possessions housed in the building were mostly boxed up.

Kathy Harrison looked at me with an expression that seemed beyond her thirty years. She looked like an old woman.

"So, Ms. Harrison, tell me about yourself." I'd gotten as comfortable as I could on the lumpy futon, which I had a sneaking suspicion was also her bed.

She seemed nervous. "I don't know what to tell. This was actually my brother's idea. He thought if we put pressure on the bank they wouldn't take the house." Fat chance. "You know, public pressure and all."

"Well, why don't you tell me what happened."

Seems Kathy Harrison lost her job at an area supermarket. Then her husband lost his job at the county -- and apparently his mind. Last week, after moving to an apartment complex a few streets over, he'd handled his job loss by barricading himself in his apartment naked.

Crap.

"You wrote the story, I think." Kathy Harrison's voice was sad and small. I couldn't help feeling sorry for her, especially when I pictured that huge hairy man lying on top of her.

I didn't really know what to say.

"I keep asking the bank if they can just give me an extension until I can get a job," she explained. "I don't think it's too much to ask. I just don't want my children to be homeless."

Looking around at the bleak surroundings, I couldn't help but wonder how much worse a homeless shelter would be.

After listening to the woes of Kathy Harrison for another half an hour, and they were many, I was pretty much done with the interview. That's when the front door opened behind me. I turned around, expecting to see one or two filthy children. Instead, I saw Rob Jones.

"Mr. Jones." What was he doing here?

"Oh, you two know each other?" Kathy seemed relieved. "Rob is my brother. He's been helping me pack up."

Small world.

"Yeah, I met Rob the other day at the county building." No sense in telling her he'd thrown water all over me.

"Rob is very upset about all of this. He's been a lifesaver. I don't know what I'd do without him."

"Good luck getting Ms. Shaw here to care," Rob fired back. "Maybe if you were wearing Ed Hardy shoes."

Asshat.

I stood up, extended my hand to Kathy Harrison, and promised her the story would run in the next few days. With a feature, you never give a hard deadline because they're the first thing to get bumped when something breaks.

"I'm sure you'll research this story with as much diligence as you did the water story and my brother-in-law's legal troubles."

I was pretty sure he was being sarcastic. The problem is, sarcasm is often wasted on me. "You can bet I will," I replied brightly.

Kathy saw me out of the house and seemed genuinely hopeful I could do something for her. I decided that I really wanted to. It wasn't her fault her husband was a nudist and her brother was a jerk.

Nineteen

After filing my story, which I spent a good two hours on, I was depressed. I see a lot of hardship in this line of work -- don't get me wrong, I see a lot of hilarious stuff, too -- but Kathy Harrison's plight had made me feel bad.

Here was this woman, raising two kids on her own, with an estranged husband who liked to run around naked with a gun.

All I had was a stalker.

The one thing I thought would make me feel better was a movie. I drove to the local Cineplex and checked the show times. Good news, the new zombie flick started in twenty minutes. Perfect timing.

Most single women would never go to a movie by themselves. I didn't have this problem. I actually prefer to go to movies by myself. Plus, I didn't know anyone that liked horror and slasher films as much as I did.

I stopped by the concession stand on my way in. I'm not a popcorn eater, but I do love my candy, even when it costs five bucks for a small bag. I'd decided on the Sour Patch Kids and a diet pop (hey, I don't want to get fat) when I felt someone move in behind me. I hate it when people invade my personal space.

I turned and came face to face with Eliot.

"What, do you have me lojacked or something?"

Eliot didn't seem deterred. "No, I didn't know you'd be here. I was just coming to see a movie."

I looked behind him, almost dreading to see whatever bimbo he'd brought to paw in the dark. There was no one there.

"Who did you come with?"

"Myself. And you?"

I don't mind going to the movies by myself. I wasn't sure I wanted to admit that to Eliot, though. He seemed to already know the answer.

"What are you seeing?"

I told him and he merely nodded. "That's what I'm seeing, too. I'm sure it won't be as good as Romero's stuff, but I'll watch it anyway."

Okay, in addition to being hot, he was a fan of George Romero. Could he be any more perfect?

I watched Eliot get a bottle of water and waited for him to order a snack. He didn't.

"Aren't you getting anything to eat?"

"Do you know how much fat is in movie popcorn?" Oh, he's one of *those* people.

"No, and I don't care." I subtlety tried to hide my Sour Patch Kids in my purse. He noticed.

We made our way into the theater. I wasn't sure if we were sitting together, or just going to the same place. Apparently we were sitting together. He led me to the middle of the theater and sat down and opened his bottle of water.

Since he'd already seen the snack, there was no way I wasn't going to eat it. I started munching on the sour-filled greatness.

"So what did you do today? Any big stories?"

I told him about Kathy Harrison. He didn't seem all that sympathetic. "Sounds rough."

"Yeah, you look real broken up about it."

"There's a lot of human suffering in the world. I can only get worked up about my own."

Something told me that Eliot didn't suffer a lot.

We avoided heavy talk after that, mostly chatting about the recent spate of horror remakes and how awful they truly were. We both agreed that *Halloween, Friday the 13th* and *A Nightmare on Elm Street* were the absolute worst while *Dawn of the Dead* and *The Texas Chainsaw Massacre* were the best before the movie started.

As I sat in the dark theater next to Eliot, I couldn't help but wonder if he'd try to make a move on me. When I found myself wishing that he would, I silently cursed myself. It was like I was in heat or something.

I tried to focus on the movie and not on Eliot's bulging biceps, but I wasn't having a lot of luck. There were zombies eating people's brains on the screen and all I could think about was Eliot's arms and what they'd feel like around me.

Finally my mind began to wander. Unfortunately, it was to what Eliot looked like naked. The movie seemed to last for ten years. When it was finally over, I was relieved.

Eliot walked me out to my car and we both stood there awkwardly for a minute. I found myself trying to prolong our time together.

"So, that was crap."

"Yeah, it really was."

"And not good crap like *People Under the Stairs*."

Eliot laughed. "I hated that movie."

"Yeah, but that's one of those movies that's so bad it's good."

Eliot conceded the point. "Like *Black Xmas*," he said with a laugh. "There's something hilariously wrong -- but in a good way -- about a little yellow guy climbing between the walls."

We both paused in an uncomfortable silence.

Eliot broke the silence first. "Do you want me to follow you home?" Yes.

"No, I'll be fine."

"Well, I'll feel better making sure you get there in one piece." I knew something that would make us both feel better.

"Well, sure."

We both got in our cars and drove to my house. The whole way there I was mentally cracking my knuckles -- and sweating my ass off. Why did he have to be so fricking hot?

When we got to the house, Eliot angled out of his pickup truck and walked with me to the front door. This was it.

I unlocked the door and turned around. I fully intended to shake his hand and send him on his merry way. No, really I did. He leaned forward and pushed the door open behind me and walked into my house.

Uh-oh.

I turned on the light and saw Eliot look around with just a hint of an amused grin. I guess you could say I'm something of a theme decorator. The living room is pretty basic, with nature scene paintings and a huge entertainment center that housed four video game systems and my DVR.

The dining room, on the other hand, features a dark wood table with *Little House on the Prairie*-like benches and a matching hutch with bright rooster dishes -- which I never ate off of. The walls were decorated in colorful New Orleans themed decor -- including a Mardi Gras mask.

"I like this art."

I liked his butt.

Eliot moved on to the kitchen, which is decorated in Disney. Floor to ceiling Disney. I even have a Mickey Mouse spoon ladle on the stove and a toaster that burns Mickey's head into the bread while spewing the "It's A Small World" theme song when the toast pos up.

Eliot didn't seem impressed. Instead, he moved back through the dining room and took a gander at my office.

This brought a smile to his face.

As something of a pack rat and book lover, I'd converted one whole wall into a bookcase by stacking wooden crates at odd angles and putting all of my *Star Wars*, *Lord of the Rings*, *Harry Potter* and *Incredible Hulk* (Bixby, not Bana or Norton) memorabilia in the crates. I'd also covered the overhead light with a large *Star Wars* flag that had a skull and crossbones on them -- only the skull was actually a stormtrooper helmet.

"This is . . . "

"Cool," I supplied.

"I was going to say the strangest thing I've ever seen in my life, but sure, I'll go with cool." I saw him staring at in the corner, where my leg lamp from *A Christmas Story* was proudly displayed.

"It looks like a movie theater threw up in here."

Eliot moved back out of the office and towards the hallway that housed my bathroom and bedroom. I unconsciously licked my lips. He was going to go in my bedroom.

He went in the bathroom first and laughed at the turtle decor. He stopped momentarily in the hallway and looked at the framed playbill from the *Buffy The Vampire Slayer: The Musical* that was on the wall. At that, he just shook his head.

The only room left was my bedroom -- and he was heading for it.

He flicked on the light as he walked in. He seemed surprised at the mundaneness of the room. I'd really never got around to decorating it. After all, the only thing I did in here was sleep.

He turned back towards me and I was practically on his heels. My only instinct was to yelp and jump away. This seemed to amuse him.

"You're not nervous are you?" Yes.

"No," I scoffed. "Why would I be nervous?"

With one stride Eliot was across the room and his tongue was in my mouth. I didn't even have time to think. Maybe I didn't want to think. I responded the way any red-blooded woman would with a hot man in her bedroom. I think I actually started panting.

I splayed my fingers across his chest -- his very impressive chest -- and as if possessed my hands started making their way down towards his pants.

His hands were roaming, too. Somehow, without my knowledge, they'd found their way under my shirt. I couldn't seem to muster up the effort to be surprised.

Eliot moved me towards the bed, pushing me to a sitting position. He stripped off his shirt as he came towards me. God, he looked even better shirtless than I imagined. His chest was decorated with a smattering of hair. Good, no manscaping, but he also wasn't an ape.

Before I knew it his tongue was in my mouth again. I found I'd missed it.

"Where are your condoms?" His voice was ragged. It took me a minute to register that he was talking to me.

"I don't have any."

He stopped and looked at me with frustration.

"Don't you have one in your wallet?" I never thought I could sound so pathetic.

"I'm not in high school, I don't generally carry them around. I keep them in the bathroom, like a normal grown-up."

"There's a Wallgreens across the road," I offered helpfully.

Eliot stood up and regarded me silently. In that moment, we both knew that by the time he got back I'd have locked the door and barricaded myself in. I think we'd both come to our senses.

Eliot pulled his shirt back over his head, defeated.

I walked him back to the front door. Part of me was relieved. The other part of me was still ridiculously turned on. I wanted to ask him to stay. Instead, I lamely said goodbye.

Eliot seemed amused again. That wasn't the reaction I was secretly hoping for.

"Don't worry. We'll have another chance at this."

I made a mental note to buy condoms the next day. Just in case, of course. I had no intention of using them.

Twenty

I woke up the next morning feeling incredibly frustrated -- both sexually and professionally.

Externally, I was glad that Eliot and I hadn't been able to get it on. Internally, I was pissed. My dreams had been filled with visions of Eliot sans his shirt. They were great dreams, until I realized that Jake was also in the room. He was holding up Olympic figure skating judging signs -- and the scores were pretty low. Then the dreams became guilt ridden. That, of course, was completely ridiculous, since I was pretty sure Jake was sowing his own wild oats with Candy.

By the time I'd showered and dressed, I realized I didn't have time for breakfast if I was going to make it to the Harrison arraignment on time. The last thing I needed was to tick off a judge -- especially given the week I was already having.

Since I was going to court, for once I dressed appropriately. No *Star Wars* shirts today. I had the sneaking suspicion that light up shoes weren't going to be welcome either. I left the house feeling kind of blah -- and only half of it was because of my dull outfit.

The Eastpointe district court has a lot in common with a war zone. The seats are wooden and hard. They also sport splinters. The walls are salmon pink and make me want to puke. It's nothing like the cozy courtrooms on the circuit court level. Hopefully I wouldn't be here long.

The first person I ran into inside the building was Kathy Harrison. She looked markedly better than the day before. The wonders a shower and nice outfit from Meijer could do.

She greeted me warmly when she saw me.

"Ms. Shaw, I want to thank you so much for the story." It must have run. "It was wonderful. I've already gotten a few calls from people who want to help."

"That's great," I enthused, and I meant it. This woman deserved any little bit of help she could get.

I noted, with a visible grimace, that she wasn't alone. Her brother had tagged along for the court proceedings.

"Mr. Jones."

"Ms. Shaw, I want to thank you for the story you wrote about Kathy," he said. "It was very well-written and truthful for a change."

A change?

"Perhaps you should stick to feature stories, since political stories seem to be above your pay grade."

Yep, still an asshole.

I smiled at Kathy as I made my way into the courtroom. I've found that engaging a jerk like Rob Jones makes you a jerk in return. I noticed, with a small sense of satisfaction, that Kathy was giving her brother a tongue lashing about his treatment of me. I knew I liked her.

When I got in the courtroom, I realized that there were only a handful of reporters in attendance. Seemed the naked dancer was already yesterday's news.

Since I didn't expect the courtroom to be crowded, I stayed away from the designated media area and sat in the general area. I wasn't in the mood for reporters today.

In typical fashion, court was late. If you've ever sat through the docket in a morning session you'd learn it's nothing like it is on television. Most of the judges work about four hours a day and they're always late getting started. Then they sit on the bench for a half an hour and take an hour-long break. Tough life.

Luckily for me, on a Thursday, there wouldn't be a lot of arraignments. I was right. After sitting through a handful of petty larceny and drunk driving cases, I finally heard the bailiff call the Harrison case up.

I didn't expect much to happen today. Evidence is pretty sparse at an arraignment. Generally, the suspect just enters a plea of not guilty and a date for a preliminary examination is set. I didn't expect this case to deviate.

I noticed that the sheriff's deputies had moved into the back of the courtroom, accompanied by a sullen Bart Harrison. I was relieved to see that he was not only dressed, but sober as well.

Most suspects seem embarrassed when brought into a courtroom. Bart was no different. He met his estranged wife's compassionate expression and looked like he wanted to cry.

Too bad he didn't think about that when I wanted to cry because I had to see him naked.

Kathy tried to move forward to talk to Bart, but I grabbed her wrist as she moved towards him.

"They're not going to let you talk to him in court."

She bit her lip to fight back tears.

"When can I see him?"

"You'll have to go to the jail."

Kathy apparently believed me. She sat down next to me and grasped my left hand. Oh, great, now she thought I was her best friend. I tried to detach my hand so I could hold my notebook. Kathy didn't seem upset about the slight.

The arraignment went pretty much how I expected. The judge ordered alcohol counseling for Bart and bail was set at $100,000, with an option for 10 percent. Sadly, for Kathy, I didn't think she could come up with the ten grand required to get her husband out. Secretly, I thought that was probably a good thing.

The case went by so quickly Kathy looked surprised when the judge got up and walked out of the courtroom. Bart was already gone.

"That was it?"

"Yeah, that was it. Court isn't really like they show it on television."

I said goodbye to Kathy, resisted the urge to shoot Rob the finger, and made my way out into the main hallway of the court building. Jake was standing outside in his dress uniform. A shot of guilt coursed through me again. I mentally slapped myself for the feeling. I didn't owe Jake anything.

"Hey."

"Hi."

We are nothing if not witty conversationalists.

"Anything happen since the last time I saw you?"

Like almost getting naked with your sworn enemy?
"No."

I couldn't tell if Jake was relieved. Part of me thought he could see the Scarlet Letter I was sure was apparent on my chest. I decided to handle the situation maturely.

"So, how's Barbie?"

"Who's Barbie?"

"Your little girlfriend. You know, Candy."

"You call her Barbie?"

I didn't want Jake to think I was jealous.

"Only because I think she's into guys who aren't anatomically correct."

That's me being mature. What can I say?

Jake shrugged off the comment. "I'm not seeing her anymore."

"Why not? Get tired of having to explain the big words in *Where The Wild Things Are?*"

"No. I just realized she's not the one for me." Was that a pointed look?

"You didn't know that when she opened her mouth?"

"I guess I'm a glutton for punishment." Another pointed look.

I didn't know what to say, so I opted for silence.

Jake was looking at his feet. He clearly wanted to say something, but was unsure of how to do it. Finally, he just went for it.

"What's the deal with you and Kane?"

I almost saw him naked last night. "Nothing."

"Nothing? Or nothing you're going to talk to me about?"

Take your pick. "Nothing."

"Do you want something to happen with him?"

Just hot sweaty sex. "No."

"Do you want something to happen with me?"

Just hot sweaty sex. Wait, what did he just say? "What?"

Jake seemed frustrated, which bothered me, since I was the confused one.

"Sometimes, when you look at me, it's like we're kids again."

"You're not going to urinate on the judge are you?"

Jake was nonplussed. "That's not what I meant."

What did he mean?

"I mean, sometimes I look at you and want to climb right back into your bed."

"We were teenagers. We rarely did it in a bed."

"Do you have to treat everything like a joke?"

He was being serious. "What do you want me to say?"

Jake grimaced.

"You said you only think of getting me in bed sometimes. What about the other times?"

"Then I want to lock you in a cell and gag you while I bang my head against the wall."

I mulled that for a moment. "Well, both sound fun."

Jake laughed at that for a moment.

"You want to be careful about Kane, you know?"

Now he was warning me off other men.

"Nothing is going on between us." Yet.

"Yeah, well . . . you want to have dinner some time?"

Dinner? Good grief.

"I don't know if that's a good idea." Mainly because I had your sworn enemy's tongue down my throat last night.

Jake seemed to think about that a second. "You're probably right."

What? He got over that idea quickly.

"Fine."

"Why are you getting so worked up?" He was playing with me now. Jerk. "Don't get your panties in a bunch."

"Don't think, even for a second, that you have any effect on my panties." Anymore. Well, hardly ever.

"I wouldn't dream of having an effect on your panties."

Scumbag.

"I think you're only interested because you think Eliot is." Sometimes, it's best to go with the truth.

"You think I'm jealous of Kane?" Jake was incredulous. I thought I'd hit the nail on the head.

"I think that may be part of it."

Jake shook his head. He appeared to be getting angrier by the second.

"You can do whatever you want with Kane. I must have been crazy to even think for a second that it would be a good idea to even consider getting involved with you again."

I think I was being maligned.

"And why is that?" I placed my hands on my hips, mimicking the best angry ex-girlfriend pose from my daily soaps. Thank you Vanessa Marcil.

"Because you're deranged, deluded and self-absorbed. All you think about is yourself. You're in your own little world where no one else can have a valid opinion -- or a real feeling. It's all about you."

Jake stalked off, he was radiating anger.

"I am not deluded!" I yelled to his retreating back.

Twenty-One

When I woke up Friday morning, I felt more wiped out than when I'd went to bed. My dreams the previous night were nothing like the erotic ones from the evening before. Instead, I spent the entire dream running between Jake and Eliot -- with Eliot turning into the Hulk and Jake turning into Darth Vader. It was really quite disturbing.

I half-heartedly showered and dressed, going for comfort in my Mark Ecko *Star Wars* hoodie, since the day looked pretty gray outside, and my simple camouflage Converse sneakers. I really didn't have the effort to dress up and annoy Fish.

I flipped through my day planner -- my one form of organization -- and saw that I didn't have anything scheduled. With any luck, I'd have to file some simple story and a few briefs for the day and then I'd be done. With family dinner looming this evening, a restful day sounded heavenly.

Instead of eating breakfast at home, I splurged on a McDonald's steak bagel on my way to work and I was feeling markedly better when I walked into the office. I noticed Marvin was in early again.

"Why are you working days again? You going to AA?"

Marvin looked exhausted. I couldn't be sure, since he always wore the same thing to work, but I think he'd slept in his clothes. The dark circles under his eyes, which were always present -- a remnant of his boxing days -- looked more haggard than usual.

"What's wrong?"

If something were legitimately wrong in Marvin's life I wanted to help him. Unfortunately, I had a feeling this was probably another manufactured drama.

"So, I was out on a date last night." This is never a good beginning for a Marvin story. I'm just issuing a warning. "She was hot. She's a dancer at the strip club down on Eight Mile. She said she was separated from her husband."

Ah, the holy trifecta for Marvin. A woman who was separated from her husband, meaning she wasn't ready for anything serious, who not only worked in the service industry, but she had the good sense to do it topless.

"We went to her house after dinner and I knew I was going to get lucky."

I nodded, feigning interest. By his own accounts, Marvin is terrible in bed. He says he's hung like an infant. I had no personal knowledge of this -- and I was thankful for it.

"So, we had a little wine." Which I'm sure went straight to both his heads. "And we moved into the bedroom."

He was rubbing his hands in anticipation right now. If he started rubbing something else, I was out of here.

"She had it all decked out."

"Decked out? What, with like candles and stuff?"

"No, with satin sheets and a whip."

Of course.

"So, we're getting into bed and she's smacking me around a little bit." Marvin must have noticed the wary look on my face. "Nothing really big, you know, just little smacks."

I didn't know, but I nodded for him to go on. Truth be told, Marvin's stories always make me laugh.

"I'm just about ready to get to Graceland." I think that means actual sex, but I'm not sure I want clarification at this point. "And then the door bursts open and it's this huge, I mean freaking huge, guy. He looked like he could be a professional wrestler."

I looked up from the mail I'd been sorting during his story and scanned Marvin's body a little closer. It didn't look like anything was broken. "Did you run away?"

"Worse."

"Did he threaten you?"

"Worse."

"Did he pull a gun?"

"Worse."

"What's worse than pulling a gun?"

"He pulled out his dick." Okay, where was this going? Oh, and that's definitely worse.

"What did he want you to do with it?" I was afraid I already knew.

"He thought we were going to have a threesome." Whoops. Turns out, Marvin's separated date was actually divorcing her husband because he was gay. This was her last ditch attempt to save the marriage.

I grimaced as Marvin explained how, since he was scared of the guy, he'd agreed to the threesome. While in the bathroom to ostensibly "freshen up," he'd tried to climb out the window and instead gotten wedged in. The fire department had ultimately been called to extract him from the window – and what little remained of his dignity.

Funnily enough, the story wasn't quite over.

"So, you think I should call her?"

"No."

"Well, I mean she's really hot."

"No."

"I don't think she's going to go back to her husband."

"No!"

Marvin looked crestfallen. I was merely annoyed.

I moved away from Marvin, I felt a little dirty myself at this point, and headed over to Fish's desk for my day's assignment. Fish seemed like he was in a good mood. Of course, it was rotary day, which meant he'd take a three-hour lunch and come back bombed. Who wouldn't be happy by that?

"Anything going on today?"

"Not much. Sheriff's department has some press release and photos of a missing woman. Do something short on it. Other than that, I left a few briefs on your desk."

Cool, easy day.

When I turned to return to my desk, I crashed into Duncan. Crap.

"So, what's the big extreme sport for next month, riding a tricycle?"

Duncan didn't seem amused. "If you must know, I'm going rock climbing."

"Where? There aren't any mountains in Macomb County. Hell, there aren't any hills."

"I'm doing it at that indoor place in the Shores."

"You mean the one where you're hooked up to cables and you climb like twenty feet up and you're done?"

"It's still very dangerous."

"How many people have died doing it?"

"None, but you can injure yourself if you fall."

"What, by getting whiplash? I think the only thing that would happen if you fell is that, in your manly terror, you'd unleash one of your little brown fighters."

If Fish hadn't been there, I'm sure Duncan would have went apeshit. However, in front of the bosses, he's always on his best behavior. Or, the best behavior he can muster.

"I'm sure someone with your limited brain capacity can't grasp the concept."

"I'm sure you're right. I can't grasp the concept of someone climbing up a rock with cables strapped to them. Why would someone who's not insane do that?"

Duncan decided arguing with me was a moot point. I couldn't agree more. As he left, Fish actually glared at his back. "That guy is such a douche."

"That's pretty much a given."

I decided to get my story done early so I could blow off the rest of the afternoon. Despite the fact that I'd probably run into Jake, I thought it best to get my visit to the sheriff's department over with quickly.

I needn't have worried. Jake was nowhere in sight and his second in command was in no mood for me to linger. He gave me the press release, the photos and a few quotes on the missing woman -- a mother of two in the ritzy northern suburbs -- and sent me on my way. I was glad to get out of the building. While part of me wanted to see Jake, the other really preferred hiding like a child. Hey, why mess with what's worked for me for the past twenty-seven years?

I stopped at the coffee shop on my way back to the office. I figured if I was going to play with fire today, I might as well do it all the way.

Upon leaving the shop, I ran into Eliot, who was walking out of the pawnshop. He smiled when he saw me.

"Miss me?"

Yes. "I was just getting some caffeine before returning to the office."

"Lucky for me, huh?"

I chose to ignore the statement.

"What are you working on today?"

"Just some missing woman from Romeo. It's a pretty easy day."

"What are you doing after work?"

"I've got a family dinner to go to." I never loved them more. From the look on his face, Eliot was ready to pick up where we'd left off the other night. I really wasn't. Okay, I really was, but I also really didn't think it was a good idea.

"And after that?"

"It's usually a three-hour extravaganza."

If he was disappointed, Eliot didn't show it. "Well, have fun."

Have fun? That's it? A little begging would be nice. A few tears. Something. Maybe I'd misunderstood his reasons for asking about my plans for the evening. "Have fun?"

"Yeah, have fun."

My brain told me to walk away -- and be cool about it.

"What are you doing tonight?" I've never been one to listen to my brain. I'm as cool as the Fonz jumping over a shark on water skis.

Eliot shrugged. "I don't know. I'll probably just go out and listen to some music or something."

Or something? I had a sneaking suspicion the "or something" was brunette and perky and she worked at the Vampire Lounge.

Eliot's gaze met mine. I didn't see any guilt hidden there. Of course, if I was being totally honest with myself, he had no reason to feel guilty. We weren't exactly betrothed to each other. Actually, we weren't exactly anything to one another but two people who'd once stuck their tongues down each other's throats.

"Well, have fun." If it worked for him it could work for me. I was as cool as Han Solo in a crisis.

"Oh, I plan to."

"Well, than you just do that." My voice sounded shrill even to my own ears.

So much for cool.

Twenty-Two

When I returned to the office, I called the missing woman's husband and listened to him fake being distraught for a half an hour. I had a sneaking suspicion that his wife wasn't missing, she was dead, and we were probably going to find her chopped up and spread out in one of the area parks in the upcoming weeks. Until then, though, she was just missing.

Marvin and I took a long lunch at the Coney place, where he went into even greater detail about his previous evening, and then returned to the office. My afternoon was filled with about twenty minutes of work and three hours of online shopping. My new Chuck Taylors were set to arrive on Tuesday.

Before leaving the office, I debated changing into something different to avoid the wrath of my mother at dinner. In typical fashion, I decided against it. If I didn't piss her off, I'm not sure we'd having anything entertaining to talk about.

Despite the overcast sky, it hadn't rained all day. The humidity of waiting for the oncoming storms was becoming oppressive. I rolled down the windows, cranked Eminem in the CD player, and let my mind wander.

In the wake of the flurry of activity in my personal life, I'd kind of let other things slide away. I realized that I hadn't received a threat, or had an attempt on my life, in almost three days. Things were looking up -- at least in that department.

On the other hand, I had a real problem in the romantic department. I couldn't deny that Jake and I would always be tied to one another, and I'd probably always be jealous of anyone else in his life. The problem was, I didn't think Jake and I could make it work.

Jake has high expectations of the people in his life. I'd never been able to live up to them. To be fair, I'd never really tried to live up to them. Sometimes it's just easier to let yourself fail than to try to succeed.

Jake, also, is bossy and a stickler for the law. I hate being bossed around and I live my life in a moral gray area most of the time. I don't see right or wrong. I see what's good and easy for me on one side and everything else on the other.

I couldn't deny that I was still attracted to Jake, but to live full time in his world -- the girlfriend of a politician -- sounded like hell on earth to me.

Then there was Eliot. I knew, without a doubt, I wanted to get Eliot into my bed. Once I did, though, what was I supposed to do with him? I didn't think Eliot was a commitment type of guy. In fact, if I had to place a wager, I'd bet he was one of those guys who had sex with a woman and then lost all interest.

Don't get my wrong, I have no problem with "no strings" sex. In fact, I didn't have a problem with "no strings" sex for the majority of my college career. The problem was, I didn't just want no strings sex with Eliot. I didn't want a relationship either, though. Where Eliot was concerned, I had absolutely no idea what I wanted. I just know I wanted him.

Of course, I wanted Jake, too.

I chewed on my lip as I debated the pros and cons of the two. Both were hot. Jake was more lean muscle, compared to Eliot's actual bulk. They were sexy in different ways, though.

Jake was successful and, though I'm loathe to admit it, patient.

Eliot radiated sex. He was successful in a different way. He didn't have a lot of patience, though, I'd wager.

Ugh. It was really an impossible choice. And, to be fair, I'm not sure I even had a choice. The only thing Eliot had offered was sex. Jake had once offered me forever -- well, a preamble to forever in the form of a promise ring -- and I'd walked away. He wasn't exactly offering me forever at this point, but what he was offering was a lot more substantial then what Eliot was offering.

Before I realized what was happening, I had reached the family restaurant. I pushed all thoughts of Jake and Eliot out of my mind. The last thing I was going to talk to my family about was my sex life. Okay, my lack of sex life in the present moment.

When I entered the restaurant, I greeted a few regulars and made my way to the family table. It looked like practically everyone in the clan had made it to dinner tonight. My mother is one of five siblings and I have fifteen cousins in varying degree of age -- I'm fairly close to the majority of my cousins who are in my age range. The three little ones kind of lost out on the cousin camaraderie. I can't be sure, but they're probably thankful for that.

When I got to the table, I immediately noticed my cousin Lexie spinning her version of the umbrella story to everyone.

"I didn't hide in the bushes," she was explaining to my mom. "I thought I dropped a contact. And when I found it, I couldn't see very well and I tripped coming out of the bushes and I just fell on her. I wasn't hitting her. It was totally an accident."

Sounded completely plausible to me.

My mother was more pragmatic. "Maybe you should try wearing glasses," she suggested helpfully.

I slid into the booth next to Lexie, choosing not to comment on her story. It's really not worth it. My mom frowned at my *Star Wars* jacket. I chose not to comment on the dirty look on her face either.

Derrick slid in on the other side of me, essentially trapping me between Lexie and himself. I didn't like the feeling.

"Anything else happen since the car thing?"

"What car thing?" My mother can smell a secret a mile away.

I glared at Derrick. He smiled. Of course he'd said it on purpose.

"I almost got hit by a car the other night. It's no big thing."

My mother frowned; I could tell she was thinking. "Were you jaywalking?" She always jumps to the explanation that blames me. When I was a teenager, the wine in the house disappeared one day. She just assumed it was me. When I told her it probably evaporated, she didn't even attempt to believe my lie.

"Yes, I was jaywalking." Seemed easier then telling the truth.

"She wasn't jaywalking." Derrick never lies. It's his biggest fault, other than being a cop, in my book. "Some guy tried to run her down outside Roseville City Hall."

"What did you do to him?" I'm sure, in my mother's mind, I'd accidentally started him on fire or something. She'd never got over the time when I was in college and my friend and I had inadvertently set the fringe on some skinhead's denim vest on fire with our lit cigarettes. She's so suspicious, even though I've clearly never earned that suspicion.

Luckily for me, everyone's attention had been diverted to the arrival of my Aunt Vera. I just want to point out that Vera and I are not related by blood. She married my Uncle Tim when I was young -- and then proceeded to cheat on him with anything that moved throughout the years. Derrick and I had often joked, behind her back of course, that she was the town bike and everyone got a ride.

For her part, Vera pretended not to notice that we all referred to her as Elvira when she wasn't around. The name stemmed from an incident a long time ago, when she and her sisters walked around the property line of her new home and chanted away evil spirits. She's always been odd -- which is something I can accept -- it's the cheating that I can't stomach.

Tonight, Vera was wearing a crochet dress -- without the shell that was supposed to go underneath it. Apparently, she thought that part of the dress was optional. Derrick and I did not.

"Do you think she knows that we don't want to see her bra and underwear while eating?"

"I'm just thankful she's wearing underwear. It could be worse." Derrick is practical in everything, I guess. When he's right, though, he's right.

Luckily for us, Vera settled down at the other end of the table.

I decided on the fish and chips for dinner and fell into the mindless chatter that accompanies a family that's as close as ours. In the middle of the table, my grandmother was telling old stories about when Derrick and I were kids. We both rolled our eyes, but humored her, interjecting the right comments where she expected us to. Yes, I was a better fisher than Derrick. Yes, it was funny when I gave Derrick a black eye. Yes, it was funny when I never let Derrick talk. I don't think either one of us liked any of the stories, just for different reasons.

After awhile, we noticed that almost everyone at the table had turned their attention to Vera. Apparently, she was spinning one of her infamous yarns. Did I mention she's a pathological liar?

Instead she was spinning one of her conspiracy theories. Even better.

"I was reading in the New York Times that all the people who disappear in the Bermuda Triangle are actually in a black hole in outer-space. Our government put them there to experiment on them."

"You read it in the New York Times?" More like the National Enquirer.

"It's the truth."

How do you argue with something like that? You don't.

"Soooo," Derrick said turning to me. "I heard all the crop circles are actually caused by farting aliens." His sense of humor springs up at the oddest times.

"Really? I heard that all those alien abductions are actually done by giant ants who take people away to their giant ant hills in the woods and make them dress up like clowns."

Vera glared at both of us. "My story is true. Your stories are just ridiculous."

The second half of the evening was pretty much identical to the first. I'll spare you the boring details. Just suffice it to say, my grandfather Jasper got caught by his nosy neighbor sleeping on the trampoline naked -- again -- and my aunt Marnie was under suspicion from local law enforcement for beheading a six-foot bunny in her former boyfriend's driveway.

"I really liked that bunny," Lexie lamented of her mother's former possession. "I called it Tibby and dressed it up when I was a kid."

"Why did she behead it?"

"Because it didn't make sense for all the fake blood to be all over it if there wasn't a big wound." Lexie was matter-of-fact.

I couldn't disagree with her logic.

Finally, I excused myself to leave. I glanced at my watch as I left the restaurant. Three hours had never felt so long. I made my way to my car, blowing out a breath of relief. I was free for another week.

I didn't notice the sound of crunching gravel behind me until whomever it was had moved practically on top of me. I prayed it wasn't Vera with a follow-up to her conspiracy theory. It wasn't.

Before I even turned around I felt something heavy come down on the back of my head. Before I lost consciousness, I registered one second of blinding pain and then I was falling into Vera's black hole.

I just hoped there was no one waiting to do experiments on me on the other side.

Twenty-Three

The pain I felt when I regained consciousness was acute. My head felt like it was double its normal size and it seemed to take me forever to focus. When I finally did, I realized I wasn't missing much.

Everything was pitch dark, except for a faint light that managed to shine through a relatively small window up near the top of the walls. I was clearly in a basement, but where?

I tried to shift my position and see if I could stand, but quickly realized that didn't seem like a reasonable option -- especially since I was tied to a support pole with my hands behind my back. Great. In addition, when I had tried to move, I'd woken up some stiff muscles that had been locked in the same position for hours and no longer wanted to move.

I grunted in pain and tried to shift again. It only seemed to make things worse.

"You finally woke up, I see."

The voice came from a couple feet behind me. It sounded familiar; I just couldn't put my finger on it. I could only hope it wasn't some deranged pervert I'd covered in a previous story.

"Who is it?"

"What, you don't recognize me? I guess that shouldn't surprise me. The only thing I'm sure about where you're concerned is that you're a spoiled bitch."

Spoiled bitch? Sounds like someone I used to date. Crap, it probably was a pervert.

"Maybe if I put on some Ed Hardy shoes?"

Crap. Not someone I used to date. Even worse.

"Rob? Rob Jones?"

"Ding, ding, ding, give the witch a prize."

"Who are you calling a witch?"

My eyes had pretty much adjusted to the darkness at this point, and I could at least make out shapes in the room. Out of the corner of my eye, I could see that Rob was pacing like a caged animal towards the far wall. He looked deranged.

"Why am I here?"

"Why are you here? Why, you're here to understand."

"Understand what?"

Rob was quiet a minute. He paused in the back and forth trail he was wearing into the rug and stalked towards me. Uh-oh. He dropped down and put his face right in front of mine, I could smell the liquor on his breath. Jack Daniels. Man, I could use a glass of that about now.

"I want you to understand that some things aren't about you."

That sounded personal. "I know not everything is about me."

"Really? Because you don't seem too concerned about people losing their jobs. You don't seem to care that people are losing their houses. You don't seem to care that the county government is screwing us."

I wouldn't say I didn't care. Like I said before, though, I was generally apathetic. I decided not to point out the difference to Rob. Something told me he wouldn't really care either way.

He was just hitting his stride anyway.

"I've been watching you."

"Well that's . . . flattering." I thought I'd try to appease him to the best of my ability. "If I was into psychos I'd totally go for you." Hey, that is to the best of my ability.

Rob chuckled. It was kind of maniacal. "You just think everyone is into you, don't you? Just because you have the sheriff and that muscle-bound idiot sniffing around, you think every guy is into self-absorbed trolls like yourself."

Trolls? This guy was asking for it.

"Well, I'm not interested in you. I prefer my women to actually have an IQ above 60."

Something told me it wasn't the time to tell Rob I'd read that IQ tests actually weren't a good gauge of intelligence.

"So, why have you been following me?" I thought it best to get him back on track. I was already getting bored.

"At first, I just wanted to scare you," Rob admitted. "After that story you wrote about Bart, I thought it would do you some good to realize the hurt you cause families and don't seem to care about. I just wanted to make you aware of your actions."

"Hey, I'm not the one who got drunk, got a gun and then got naked. How is that my fault?"

"Bart didn't hurt anyone!" Rob was getting angry. Of course, since the day I'd met him, I'd known he was an angry guy.

"Hey, if it's any consolation, Bart will probably only do like a year in prison since they're so overcrowded. They'll give him some counseling there and he'll probably be better off than when he went in." This was, of course, if he managed to avoid being someone's bitch while incarcerated.

"Better off? Even when he gets out everyone will know. Everyone will know what he did."

I decided to change tactics. "Well, that's not my fault. I didn't make him do it. And, you seem to forget, I wasn't the only media there. Why not go after them?"

"Like I said, at first I only wanted to scare you. Unlike the other reporters, you were dumb enough to be listed in the phone book. It wasn't until I met you that I decided I wanted to hurt you."

Believe it or not, this is not the first time I've heard that.

"I watched you for days. I watched you waste your life. I mean, seriously, who can spend as much time as you do playing video games?" Only someone truly dedicated.

"Even tonight, with your family, you seemed disinterested. Why is that? You have a large family. You should be thankful you have so many people that care."

"They don't all care," I corrected him without thinking. "Some of them care and some of them are just plain crazy."

Rob glowered at me. "I see your judgmental ways aren't just reserved for strangers."

Despite how calm I probably seemed to Rob, I was starting to panic. He was eerily controlled. Given the times I'd seen him fly off the handle, I didn't think this was a good thing.

"So, what are you going to do to me?"

Rob, who had seemed lost in thought for about thirty seconds, snapped back to regard me. "I'm going to kill you, of course."

My mouth went dry and I swear I thought my eyes were going to roll back into my head. For a second, I thought I was going to lose consciousness again. Something in me stopped that from happening, though. I was certain if I blacked out, I'd never wake up.

I finally regained the ability to talk, unfortunately my voice sounded terrified -- even to my own ears. "Why are you going to kill me? What good is that going to do?"

Rob seemed relaxed as he regarded me. "Well, I thought about it. The county didn't react to my water demonstration. The cops didn't seem to care even when Bart went off the deep end. Then, when you wrote that story about my sister, Kathy, I thought that people would understand now. I thought everyone would join together and we'd stop the county from what they were doing. Now, I think it's going to take a dead body to get my point across."

Okay, I may be scared, but I'm not stupid. That seemed like some circular reasoning to me. Rob wasn't dedicated to a cause, he was just nuts.

"You're willing to kill someone about water rates?"

Rob snapped. "It's not just about water rates! It's about our politicians thinking they're above everyone else. They think that they don't have to give up anything and we can just give and give and give and never stop. They took away my job because I uncovered the fact that they were funneling money out of the water department and using it for their own vacations." Ah, the missing $500,000. I couldn't wait to nail Clara Black on that.

"I'm not a politician."

Rob fixed his crazy eyes on me. "No, you're not a politician. But you represent them. You speak for them. You act like them." That was just insulting.

Rob quietly moved over to me. It was then that I noticed that he had a knife in his hand. I desperately pushed against the floor with my feet and as I shoved myself backwards. I felt the ropes around my wrists loosen slightly. Of course, in my terror, I could have been imagining it.

"We're in the basement of your sister's house aren't we?" I was grasping at straws. "If you kill me here they'll track it back to you." If we weren't at Kathy's house, then I was screwed.

Rob seemed to stop and consider that for a moment. "You're right." Whew. "I can't get blood all over the place. I'm going to have to strangle you."

What? I shoved myself back against the ropes again and felt them give even more. A little bit more and I could pull one of my hands loose. It would probably hurt like hell, but it was still better than being strangled.

"If you strangle me, you'll leave fingerprints." I probably shouldn't keep helping him get away with my murder, I thought. "And you know Jake Farrell. He won't stop until he gets his man."

For a second, my heart stopped when I said it. Would Jake be the one to identify my body? My heart ached at the thought.

Rob smiled at me. "Good idea. Thanks. I've got gloves upstairs." Great.

As soon as Rob moved up the stairs, I desperately started wriggling around and continued to loosen the ropes. I could hear Rob moving around on the floor above. I knew I only had one chance at this. I had to make it count.

I gritted my teeth and pulled. Hard. I could feel my left hand come free -- leaving a lot of skin behind as it did. I wanted to cry out but I stopped myself from doing it. I couldn't alert Rob to the fact that I was loose.

I managed to climb to my feet despite the pain that was registering from my aching muscles. I wobbled and almost toppled over, but instead I grabbed the support pole I'd been tied to and regained my footing. Both of my legs were full of pins and needles. They felt alien. I started for the stairs anyway. I probably looked like I was drunk. I suddenly wished I was. When you're drunk, you're too stupid to be scared.

Somehow, I made my way up the stairs. Luckily for me, there was a door right at the top. Just as I started to open it, I realized the burglar chain was engaged. Crap. Rob would hear it clang. I was able to stop the door mid-swing and slid the chain off. I opened the door and exited into the dark backyard.

I managed to keep my wits about me enough to close the door quietly behind me. If Rob didn't notice the chain was off the door, I would gain a few seconds while he went back into the basement. Those few seconds could make the difference.

I scanned to my right and left. The house on the right was dark, but I did notice that, about four houses down, there was a bonfire going and what looked to be a group of people milling about it. Problem was, each yard was cut off with a chain-link fence.

I had two choices. I could yell out and alert not only them but Rob to the fact that I was in the backyard. Or, I could try to get in the front yard and run down the street. I decided on the latter.

I moved to the front of the fence, looking for a gate. I couldn't find one. Crap. I started to move back towards the other side of the yard when the back door flew open and Rob stood illuminated in the doorway in a scene from every horror movie I'd ever watched. He was carrying his knife again.

Double crap.

I tried to yell out, but the terror had sucked my voice into oblivion. Instead, I turned back and tried to launch myself over the fence. I was halfway over when Rob reached me. I kicked out with the leg that still remained on the other side of the fence and, against all odds, I managed to make contact with his face. He grunted and swung out with the knife, which ripped into my ankle painfully. This time I did manage to cry out. I had no idea, though, if the people down at the fire had heard me.

With a hard thud I landed on the other side of the fence, the wind momentarily knocked out of me. My ankle screamed in pain and I could feel the blood seeping from it. I didn't have a chance to sit and think about it, though. I willed myself to my feet despite the dull throb in my ankle that turned into a screaming ache when I gained my footing and moved towards the street. Adrenaline is a great equalizer. I just kept thinking that if I could just make it to the street then I would be safe.

I staggered forward, urging myself not to take the time to look back to see where Rob was. Just focus on what's in front of you, I told myself. I didn't listen. I turned back and was horrified to realize that Rob was not only over the fence, he was closing in on me.

My ankle was screaming at me to stop. So I began to run. I was only a foot from the road when another dark figure came out of the darkness and I ran headlong into him. Whoever it was managed to grab me before I fell backward.

"Are you alright?"

I'd never been so happy to see a stranger in my entire life. "No," I gasped. "He's trying to kill me."

Under the light, I finally got a chance to see my savior. He was about 6-feet tall, with a baldhead, huge beer gut and tattoos everywhere. I was pretty sure he was some sort of biker given the leather vest he was wearing.

"He's not going to hurt you, honey."

It was then that I realized, he wasn't alone. He'd brought five of his closest friends with him -- and one of them was carrying a bike chain.

Rob must have noticed the new participants -- and registered their absolute girth -- because he'd decided that killing me was nowhere near as important as saving himself. He started to run in the opposite direction. He didn't get very far.

Five bikers descended on him -- and proceeded to beat the crap out of him -- while he screamed like a little girl.

I couldn't muster a lot of sympathy for him.

Twenty-Four

It seemed the biker gang lived by a code. Women were not to be touched but men were open season. By the time the cops had arrived, I was sure that Rob wished he'd just stabbed me in the basement.

The paramedics who'd checked me over and stitched me up on-scene declared I was lucky that the injury was so minor. Yeah, that's what I felt, lucky, twice in one week.

I wasn't surprised when, about twenty minutes later, Jake appeared at the scene. He was making his way through the crowd with a purpose. A purpose that was clearly me. When he caught sight of me, he blew out a sigh of relief as he raced over.

"Are you okay?"

"Yeah, I'm fine." I was not going to cry, not matter how badly I wanted to.

Jake read the emotion behind my eyes and silently wrapped his arms around me. He hid me from prying eyes as I began to sob uncontrollably. He looked uncomfortable with my show of emotion, but to his credit, he didn't say anything.

After a few minutes, I regained control and pushed away from him.

"So what happens to Rob now?"

"Rob is going away for a long time," Jake said soothingly. "I don't think he'll be throwing water on anyone any time soon."

Throwing water? What about terrorizing with a knife?

"Are you going to be okay for a few minutes?" he asked. "I want to go talk to some of the officers."

I waved him off. The close proximity was too much for me. I was relishing a few minutes alone to collect myself. So, of course, that's when Eliot arrived. He must live his life with that police scanner on.

He walked up to Jake and they spoke for a few minutes, although I couldn't make out what they were saying to each other. Ultimately, Jake gestured over to me and Eliot made his way across the yard, to where I was sitting alone.

"Hey kid. So, what did you do tonight?"

I couldn't help but laugh at Eliot's lightweight banter. It was just what I needed. He was kind of like the Han Solo to Jake's more responsible Luke Skywalker.

"Nothing much to speak of. Just a normal night for me."

"That's what I'm afraid of," Eliot admitted ruefully. He tousled my hair affectionately. "Well, at least this chapter in the Avery Shaw disaster book is finished. How long until the sequel?"

Disaster?

Hmph.

□

A couple days later, I was pretty much back to my regular self. My ankle was still sore, but it could hold the majority of my body weight. I wasn't ready to take on rogue Sith agents on my Wii yet, but I was getting there.

I hadn't been back to work, but Marvin had called to tell me that once the story had broke, hundreds of people had call in to offer their support -- to Kathy. In fact, a local developer had stepped in to offer her a new house free and clear. Another small business owner had given her a job.

Despite everything, I was happy for Kathy. It wasn't her fault her brother was a nut-job and her husband had been driven to the brink of his own sanity. Hopefully, things would start looking up for her from this point on.

In addition, one of the other reporters at the paper had followed up on my Clara Black tip about the missing money and there was a huge political scandal brewing. One someone else got to cover -- and get the credit for.

During my forced home seclusion, I also hadn't heard from Jake or Eliot. I was torn on the issue. Part of me wondered why they couldn't even be bothered to send flowers, or a *Lego Star Wars* set. The other was just thankful I'd have the time to regain my strength before I had to deal with either of them. I was pretty sure I'd need my full arsenal to deal with that whole situation.

That was a fight for another day.

Lando had stopped by, though. He brought a gift he thought I'd love -- and it had nothing to do with *Star Wars*. Instead, it was the much sought after *Silent Hill* game -- a whole two weeks before it was released.

Life is good.

So, for the time being, I was perfectly happy to camp out on my couch with my collection of horror movies -- the *Friday the 13th* collection was currently in -- a new video game and my stuffed Yoda as the only male figure I needed in my personal space.

Author's Note

I want to thank everyone who took the time to read my debut novel. Like any author, I look back on this book and am filled with warm memories. I think I learned a lot from writing it, and hopefully I will get better as time goes on.

If you liked the book, please take a few minutes and leave a review. I understand that my characters aren't for everyone. These are not bright and shiny people

Made in the USA
Lexington, KY
02 April 2013